THE MIAMI ... ER

All o... ...Parker Garciety is ... ...way. South the une... ...t eligible of hote... ...elor is not about to Garrison ...on't let his company fold. The be long until the vultures eldest Garrison has been begin circling. seen making the rounds about town with a new woman in tow—some say it's his personal assistant, but we don't remember her being that attractive. What does Parker have up his sleeve…and how soon will all hell break loose?

Sources close to the family say the patriarch has left his brood in total disarray. There is talk of a second wife and possibly another heir to the Garrison dynasty. His company's investors are grumbling, and the Garrison brand has been irreparably tarnished. And stiff competition from the Jefferies clan threatens to disband what's left of the Garrison empire.

Dear Reader,

There is nothing quite like the culture, color and romance of south Florida. The sidewalks of South Beach sizzle with the beautiful people, the nightclubs rock with excitement and the sun soaks everything in a golden glow. I know because I've lived in Florida for almost fifteen years, and for much of that time, I worked in Miami and played on the narrow strip of land known simply as SoBe. Because of that, I am thrilled to launch a new dynasty series that is as hot as the tropics and as cool as the neon lights on Ocean Avenue.

In many ways, the Garrison family is typical of the über-wealthy, ultrachic, super-hip residents of South Beach, but they are also men and women with dreams and disappointments, fears and frustrations. And because their stories are part of the Desire line, the characters are as rich with conflict as they are with cash. And, best of all, they have secrets that threaten to tumble their empire, or break their hearts.

I fell in love with all the Garrisons, as I hope you will. In this series, you can root for the alpha men, like Parker Garrison, who sometimes lose the control they cherish, and cheer for the lucky ladies, like Anna Cross, who threaten to wreck the order of the men's lives. So grab a pastel-colored drink, dig your feet into some imaginary sand and discover the world of power, privilege and passion that is the Garrison family of Miami Beach!

Roxanne St. Claire

ROXANNE ST. CLAIRE

THE CEO'S SCANDALOUS AFFAIR

Published by Silhouette Books

America's Publisher of Contemporary Romance

Special thanks and acknowledgment are given to Roxanne St. Claire for her contribution to THE GARRISONS miniseries.

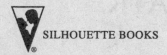

SILHOUETTE BOOKS

ISBN-13: 978-0-373-76807-3
ISBN-10: 0-373-76807-9

THE CEO'S SCANDALOUS AFFAIR

Books by Roxanne St. Claire

Silhouette Desire

Like a Hurricane #1572
The Fire Still Burns #1608
When the Earth Moves #1648
The Highest Bidder #1681
The Sins of His Past #1702
The Intern Affair #1747
The CEO's Scandalous Affair #1807

ROXANNE ST. CLAIRE

is an award-winning, national bestselling author of more than a dozen romance and suspense novels. Her first book for Silhouette Desire was nominated for a prestigious RITA® Award from the Romance Writers of America, and she is also a recipient of the 2005 Maggie Award as well as multiple Awards of Excellence. In addition, her work has received numerous nominations for a variety of awards, including a SIBA Award for Best Fiction of 2005, a National Reader's Choice Award and a Booksellers Best Award. Roxanne's first book was published in 2003, after she spent nearly two decades as a public relations and marketing executive. Today she writes full-time, while raising two preteen children and enjoying life with a real-life alpha hero. She lives on the east coast of Florida and loves to hear from readers through e-mail at roxannestc@aol.com and snail mail, c/o of the Space Coast Authors of Romance, P.O. Box 410787, Melbourne, Florida 32941. Visit her Web site at www.roxannestclaire.com to read excerpts, win prizes and learn more!

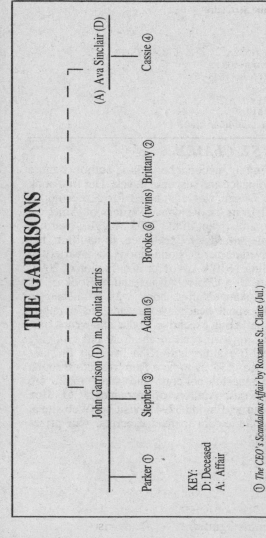

THE GARRISONS

John Garrison (D) m. Bonita Harris

---- (A) Ava Sinclair (D)

Parker ① | Stephen ③ | Adam ⑤ | Brooke ⑥ (twins) Brittany ② | Cassie ④

KEY:
D: Deceased
A: Affair

① *The CEO's Scandalous Affair* by Roxanne St. Claire (Jul.)
② *Seduced by the Wealthy Playboy* by Sara Orwig (Aug.)
③ *Millionaire's Wedding Revenge* by Anna DePalo (Sept.)
④ *Stranded with the Tempting Stranger* by Brenda Jackson (Oct.)
⑤ *Secrets of the Tycoon's Bride* by Emilie Rose (Nov.)
⑥ *The Executive's Surprise Baby* by Catherine Mann (Dec.)

One

When Parker Garrison strode into the conference room of Garrison, Inc., he noticed three things, despite the blinding sunshine that bounced off the water of Biscayne Bay and silhouetted the figures of his siblings, their mother and a few highly paid lawyers. One, there was no conversation. None. Not that he'd expected a party atmosphere at the reading of his father's will, but it was unusual for a gathering of Garrisons to be quiet. They were, at the very least, an opinionated clan.

Two, his mother appeared relatively sober. All right, it was eight-thirty in the morning and even Bonita Garrison rarely hit the juice before noon, unless he counted the Bloody Marys she consumed in preparation for the Sunday family dinners. But since his father's death two weeks ago, she'd leaned on her liquid crutch early and often.

Three—and most significant—John Garrison's chair at

the head of the mile-long cherrywood table remained empty. A situation Parker intended to rectify.

His sister Brittany practically choked when he eased himself onto the buttery leather and set his BlackBerry on the table in front of him.

"You're sitting in Dad's chair?" Brittany demanded, tapping the digital device that was never far from his right hand.

"It's empty." Parker ignored the implication that he was muscling in on his father's turf. Because he *was*. He was the oldest. He'd run the family's umbrella corporation for the past five years, since his father had given him the CEO position as a thirty-first birthday present.

The rest of them had their hands deep in the Garrison affairs—they each owned one of the properties, whether it was the Grand hotel, a club, restaurant or condo complex. But he'd earned this chair, and not just by birth order. With work, sweat, insight, guts and a few masterful decisions.

"It's disrespectful," Brittany hissed, tapering her brown eyes in disgust and leaning her narrow shoulders closer to make her point. "To the dead."

Brooke reached over and touched her sister's hand. "Relax, Britt. He has to sit somewhere."

Parker threw a grateful glance at his other sister, marveling at how the sisters were twins in appearance only. Brooke responded with a smile that softened her lovely features and accentuated the difference between the sweet sister and the scowling one even more.

Across from Brooke and Brittany, Stephen locked his hands behind his head and rocked his chair easily with a long, muscular body that practically matched Parker's gene for gene, right down to the signature cleft that every Garrison sported on their chin. Stephen's dark eyes danced with wry amusement, his flawless smile white against a face tanned from a recent escape on his sixty-foot cabin cruiser.

"Sit wherever you like, big brother," Stephen drawled. "He may not be using the chair, but I think we're about to feel the hand of our dearly departed father in every corner of this room."

Parker frowned at the comment, and followed his closest sibling's meaningful gaze to the imposing figure cut by Brandon Washington, the young and brilliant attorney who handled the family affairs. Brandon's strong jaw was set as he moved papers purposefully in front of him, his large hands steady and determined. At that moment, he met Parker's gaze, and just beneath the burnish of his espresso-colored complexion, Parker could see…anger? Surprise? Dread?

Whatever Brandon had read in John Garrison's will, the warning look the lawyer gave Parker held a clear message: *You're not going to like this.*

Parker shifted in his seat, tamping down concern. What could the will say that Parker wouldn't like? Nothing mattered to him except control of Garrison, Inc. The money, the properties, the estate—all were secondary to him, all one notch less important than the umbrella firm that invested the profits.

Let the others have their slices of responsibility. He held the biggest piece of the pie dish in his hand. Surely Dad wouldn't have changed his mind about a decision he'd made five years ago, long before he'd known he'd die at sixty-two from a heart attack.

Still, he really didn't like the vibe Brandon emitted. And neither, he could tell, did his mother.

Evidently, Bonita Garrison had picked up the same message, her fragile features drawn from mourning and worry. She pushed at an imaginary strand of jet-black hair, a silver thread catching the light, the gesture one of pure nervousness as she studied Brandon for clues. Were there surprises in store for her today? Hadn't she discussed every aspect of John's last will and testament with the man she'd married more than thirty-seven years earlier?

Maybe not, judging by the quiver of her delicate hands. Maybe she *should* have had a slug of Stoli before they'd gathered. Hell, maybe this event called for a round for the table. If only to numb the still-raw pain caused by losing a man deeply loved by each of his five children. A love, Parker thought bitterly, that didn't exactly extend to their cool and distant mother.

Adam arrived last, the only missing sibling of the five, slipping into the conference room in his usual quiet, detached way, shaking back some of his long, dark hair. He'd have to see a barber if he wanted to be taken more seriously than just the owner of a nightclub—even if Estate was one of Miami Beach's hottest spots. As birth order would have it, Adam was the youngest of the three Garrison men, but sat dead center in the family once the twins came along to claim the joint spot as "babies."

When the lawyer cleared his throat and stood, Parker ended his musings about his family. They'd all work out their various issues and problems, he felt certain. And he'd work out his problems—like the current decline in the Garrison brand that translated into unhappy investors, business partners and patrons.

He'd solve that, as long as he had the lion's share of control. He turned his attention to Brandon with the confidence of a man who rarely lost his focus. That legendary focus had gotten Parker where he was today, and it would keep him there far into the future.

Hadn't Dad assured him of that?

Brandon droned legalese. Next to him, Stephen shot a look of impatience to Parker, who curled his lip in a half smile of response. Brittany doodled on a pad, tempting Parker to kick her under the table and tell his flighty little sister to pay attention. Brooke watched the lawyer, rapt, as did Adam. His mother shifted in her seat, and sighed under her breath as assets were divided and doled exactly as they had all expected.

Suddenly, Brandon stopped talking. He inhaled slowly. He looked at Bonita with no small amount of pity and then leveled his gaze directly at Parker.

"The next section is in regard to the controlling shares of the parent company, Garrison, Inc. Mr. Garrison stated that they are to be divided among his six children."

Parker flinched. Brittany blinked. Stephen leaned forward, uttering a quiet, "What?"

Did he say *six?*

The lawyer must be putting in too many billable hours.

"Uh, there are five of us, Brandon," Parker corrected, a little smile tugging at his lips. "See?" He crooked his head toward the table. "Five."

Brandon responded with a long, silent stare, underscored by a nervous laugh from one of his young associates.

"Five in this room," Brandon said deliberately. "Six in all."

For a split second, no one said anything as shock rolled off the room's residents, bounced all over the table and left a palpable change in the air. Parker scowled at the lawyer, trying to process what he'd said.

Then chaos erupted when Stephen bellowed, "That's preposterous!" and Brittany let out a surprised shriek and Brooke half stood to demand an explanation. Through it all, their mother breathed so hard she damn near growled. Only Adam was quiet, but even he wore an expression of complete disbelief.

Brandon held up a hand, but they ignored him. The noise level rose, the undercurrent of incredulity and fury elevated with each question and demand.

"Stop!" Parker said with a solid *thwack* on the cherry-wood. "Let him finish."

As it had for most of his thirty-six years, a single command brought his younger siblings in line. When the room was finally silent, he said, "Obviously, this begs for an explanation."

Brandon nodded and read from the document. "The controlling shares of Garrison, Inc. will be divided among my six..." he paused and raised an eyebrow for emphasis "...children. The division is as follows—fifteen percent, in equal shares, to Stephen, Adam, Brooke and Brittany."

Parker's chest tightened as he waited for Brandon to continue.

"The remaining forty percent will be split evenly between my son Parker and my daughter Cassie Sinclair, who will also be given full ownership of the Garrison Grand-Bahamas property."

Blood sang in Parker's head nearly as loudly as the eruption that filled the room again.

"Cassie Sinclair is his daughter?"

"The manager of the Bahamas property now owns it?"

"And twenty percent of the parent company?"

"She's not his..."

Bonita Garrison stood slowly, her face ghost-white, her hands quaking. Her children quieted, as all eyes turned toward her.

"The son of a bitch," she said to no one in particular. "The cheating son of a bitch. I'm glad he's dead."

She pivoted and walked out of the room, her shoulders quivering as she tried to hold them square. A barrage of questions, accusations and outraged calls for the truth exploded in her wake.

Now, Parker thought bitterly, it sounds like a typical Garrison family gathering.

But his pulse drowned it all out, and he had to physically work to control a temper he'd long ago conquered.

No damn wonder Brandon had given him that silent warning. And no damn wonder his father had stayed so deeply involved in the day-to-day operations of the Bahamas property.

"Who'd have guessed that?" Stephen said to him, softly enough so only Parker could hear. "The old man had someone on the side."

Parker closed his eyes in disgust. Not because his father had had an affair. And not because that sin had created a sixth Garrison child. But because, for some reason he'd never know or understand, John Garrison had decided to slice Parker's world in half, and give the other portion to some hotel manager living in Nassau.

Some hotel manager—now *owner*—who was his half sister.

He pushed his chair away from the table, determined not to let the bubble of anger brew into a full boil. Instead, he cut his gaze to Brandon's, ignoring the chaos around them.

"We'll talk, Brandon," Parker said. "But I've got a company to run."

Brittany let out a tiny snort. "You have *part* of a company to run."

He refused to dignify the comment, but scooped his PDA off the table, nodded to Stephen in particular and the table in general. "Knock yourselves out, kids."

Without waiting for a response, he left the room, grateful that unlike the rest of them, who would have to travel to various Garrison properties, his office was just down the hall on the twenty-second floor of the Brickell Avenue high-rise that housed the corporate offices of Garrison, Inc.

There, he would find sanctuary and maybe the privacy to sucker punch a wall with no witnesses.

He'd tell Anna to hold every call and appointment. What he needed to do was assess the situation and figure out a solution. That was what he did. Cold, calculating and calm, Parker Garrison manipulated every move of a multimillion-dollar empire, so he could certainly control his insanely bad mood and maybe his father's ridiculously poor judgment.

He ignored the provocative smile of Sheila, the heavily made-up receptionist who manned the front desk of the plush executive offices of Garrison, Inc. He continued directly to his corner office, resisting the urge to rip off his tie and howl in fury, his blood temperature rising with each purposeful stride toward privacy.

As he turned the corner, he expected to see his assistant at her desk, efficiently gatekeeping his world as she'd been doing for a few months since he'd promoted her from the human resources department. But Anna's desk was empty, with no sign of light or life.

At nine in the morning?

Wasn't anything the way it was supposed to be today?

Inhaling sharply, he pushed the door to his office open and closed it without giving in to the temptation to slam it, swearing softly on his exhale.

That was when he heard the humming. Not a normal hum of activity or a printer or even the refrigerator from the wet bar in the corner. No, this was more like a screaming buzz. But that wasn't all. The humming barely drowned out…

Singing.

He paused for a minute, then looked toward the source, behind the partially opened bathroom door discreetly tucked around the corner of his spacious office. Singing?

If you could call that *singing*. More like a sinfully off-key soprano belting out something from…*West Side Story*. She felt pretty? Oh, so pretty? It was hard to tell with the whine as loud as a jet engine drowning it out, and the total flatness of the notes.

Propelled by curiosity and still fueled by a losing battle with his temper and control, he continued toward the sound, the soft warmth of shower steam tumbling from the open door, along with something that smelled like flowers and powder.

He paused at the eight-inch gap in the bathroom door, leaned in to be sure he wasn't imagining things, then just stood there and stared at…

Legs.

No. That didn't do them justice. These were works of art. Heaven-sent. Endless, bare, tight-thighed, smooth-skinned, strip-club worthy legs spread about a foot apart, slipped into three-inch heels and topped off by a barely covered-in-silk female rump stuck straight in the air.

He gaped, mesmerized and only slightly deafened by the noise, which was caused by a blow-dryer aimed at a cascade of dark hair that hung upside down and grazed the marble floor of his private bathroom.

She couldn't sing her way out of a paper bag, but if he

stood here listening and looking too much longer, he'd *need* a paper bag for hyperventilation.

Suddenly, she jerked to a stand, whipped her still-damp hair over her shoulder and faced the mirror, giving him a wide-open shot of a pink lace bra that barely covered her sweetly curved cleavage.

"Oh, my God!" She yelped and spun around, slapping her hands over her and hardly covering a thing. His gaze dropped lazily, taking in the narrow waist, the flare of feminine hips, the low bikini cut of delicate pink panties cupping an alluring apex between those lovely thighs.

Good God, his administrative assistant had been hiding all this under navy pantsuits and crisp white blouses?

"Anna?" His voice sounded as tight as his throat suddenly felt.

"What are you doing here?" she demanded.

The question yanked him back to her face, her appealing features tinged with the shade of her matching underwear, bottle-green eyes bright with embarrassment.

"What am *I* doing here?" He didn't mean to smile. Or stare. But, he was human. And she was…unbelievable. "Last time I checked, this was my office."

She managed an indignant breath—no mean feat for a woman clad only in heels and underwear. "I mean, so soon. What are you doing here so soon? Aren't you in a meeting? With your family? About the will?"

The will. The words whacked him over the head as effectively as if he'd stepped into the shower that still dripped behind her. "I left early."

She threw a pleading glance at the towel rack next to him. She wanted coverage. But he wanted answers. And a few more seconds to memorize every delectable inch of her.

"I wasn't expecting you," she said, still struggling for her always-professional voice.

"No kidding." He couldn't help the tease in his. This was, without a doubt, the bright spot in an otherwise dismal morning.

"I went running," she said, with another desperate look at the towel rack. "It's very humid out there. I needed a quick shower. I thought you'd be a while."

His gaze was slipping again, along with his ability to form a coherent thought other than the one screaming in his brain: How the hell had his all-business-all-the-time administrative assistant concealed that body from him?

And why would she? Most women with a figure like hers would wear as little as possible, as often as they could.

"The meeting ended early," he said calmly, lingering just one more minute on the heels. Did she wear them every day?

He tore his attention from her slender ankles to slide over the neat little turn of her calf and meander back to that silky triangle with a silent vow to buy more Victoria's Secret stock. He zeroed in on a luscious inny navel, then paused just long enough for those lace cups to rise and fall with an exasperated breath.

"If you don't mind, I could use a towel." Her demand was sharp as shock morphed into anger.

She was angry? He should give her a lesson in professionalism, a reminder that she shouldn't be making herself at home in his office. He could treat her like the employee she was, and reprimand her for not being at her desk, or even issue a warning that she shouldn't assume anything about his schedule.

But all he did was smile and tug the towel from the rack, holding it out to her. "Great shower, isn't it?"

Her eyes widened in surprise as she took the welcome cover and wrapped it around her narrow frame, hiding every blood-warming curve. "Yes."

"Gotta love those dual massage heads."

A sneaky smile pulled at her mouth as she tucked terry into terry and formed a makeshift knot under her collarbone.

"Yes. They're great. Both of them." She straightened and lifted her chin, doing her very best to appear the altogether competent assistant who'd impressed him from the first interview. She almost pulled it off, except for the tumbling waves of dark hair that she normally wore in a tight twist, and the fact that the towel barely covered her backside.

He cleared his throat and tried really hard to scowl. "Anna," he said sternly.

"Yes?"

His head pounded with the morning's news followed by the surprise attack on his hormones. But that was no reason to take his anger and physical response out on this young woman whose only real crime was bad timing. Or good timing, depending on your perspective.

"Don't quit your day job to be a singer."

Her smile transformed her whole face, taking what had been plain, passably pretty features to something more stunning. "Not to worry, Mr. Garrison."

But he was worried. Not only had he missed her incredible body, he'd never even noticed her milky smooth skin, or the way the tip of her tongue slipped between her teeth when she smiled, or how nicely her eyes tilted up at the sides. He'd never noticed this lovely woman right under his nose.

So of course he worried. Worried that he was going blind. Or maybe he was just so deep into the family business that he'd failed to see the gorgeous woman who sat outside his office all day long.

He turned to leave, closing the door to give her privacy to dress, and congratulating himself on the return of control and focus. And perspective.

So she was pretty. So she had a body that could bring him to his knees. It didn't matter. What had just happened was nothing more than a close encounter that she would regret and he would forget. She was an excellent assistant and he had an empire to run, a will to contest, a brand to build. He needed his legendary control and focus more than ever.

But, damn, it would be hard to forget those legs.

Anna crossed the Oriental rug that welcomed visitors to the CEO's suite and stabbed the digital air conditioner control until it read a chilly sixty-seven degrees.

But even that wouldn't reduce the burn of embarrassment that singed her from the roots of her hair to the tips of her toes. If it even *was* embarrassment. It was a burn, anyway. As hot and uncomfortable as Parker Garrison's eyes when he'd given her a visual lick from those same roots to those same toes.

A familiar wicked, gooey sensation stirred low in her belly. Really low. Really wicked. Really familiar. And really *dumb* to think about her boss that way.

"Stupid," she chided as she turned on her computer and picked up the phone receiver to listen to voice mail messages. How could she have been so careless? Just for five extra minutes under the ultimate hydro-jet massage from heaven?

God, if he knew how many times she'd treated herself to that shower, she'd be updating her résumé. And she'd worked in human resources long enough to know that the last place she wanted to be was on the job market. No one hired anyone without a check of the Internet—and she knew exactly what would pop up when someone typed "Anna Cross" into a search engine.

Accused of corporate spying...

No, Anna shouldn't do anything that would force her to look for another job. So, she'd better hope her boss didn't think borrowing the shower was grounds for dismissal.

She squeezed her eyes shut as she listened to the voice mail system announce that Parker Garrison had seventeen messages.

Seventeen? What the heck was going on?

By the time she jotted down message number five, she knew. At least she knew that something really bad had gone down at the morning meeting. The various Garrison siblings and a couple of lawyers didn't provide details in their voice mails, but their tone, along with a few clues about "what the will said," didn't sound good.

Parker's door had remained firmly shut since she'd done her level best to exit his office with some measure of dignity, knowing he watched her, knowing he'd seen *everything* she'd been careful to hide. Ever since she'd arrived at Garrison, Inc. four years ago, Anna had done whatever was necessary to stay off the radar, and do an outstanding job as an administrative assistant.

In fact, she'd done such an outstanding job in human resources that she'd been handed the promotion of her dreams when the slot for Parker Garrison's administrative assistant had become available three months ago. Maybe, considering her history, she should have turned it down.

But she couldn't resist the upgrade in status, pay and benefits. Plus, she'd been tucked away on a lower floor for almost four years. Surely, after all this time, her past would remain, well, in the past.

Still, it had become habit to keep a low profile.

Until ten minutes ago when her profile had been anything but low. It had been…damn near naked.

She closed her eyes again as another heat wave threatened, trying to ignore it as she noted each caller. No, that definitely wasn't embarrassment. Nor was it a feminine response to the warmth of Parker's very obviously high opinion of how she looked sans suit. The heat wave that warred with the air conditioner was raw terror.

The only thing she'd ever wanted out of this job, this city and this life was anonymity and peace. No attention—from men or media. No connection—with her boss or his associates. No trouble—ever. And what had just happened in that bathroom spelled *attention, connection* and *trouble* in capital red letters.

She recorded the rest of the messages on a call sheet that she delivered to him hourly, only slightly reassured by the fact that whatever was going wrong in Parker's world, it would divert his attention from her.

Her intercom buzzed.

"Yes, Mr. Garrison?"

"I need you."

Her gut clenched. "I'll be right there, Mr. Garrison."

"I think, Anna—" his voice in the receiver was just soft enough to make her tighten her grasp and push the phone closer to her ear "—you could probably call me Parker now."

Now that I've seen you in your underwear. Her heart wobbled. "Absolutely, Mr.…Parker."

He was still chuckling when she hung up.

"Come on, Anna," she whispered to herself, gathering her planner and pen. Parker didn't strike her as the kind of man to torture and tease a woman, or one who would

assume that just because he'd seen her in the almost altogether that he could have his way with her.

She stood, surprised at how shaky that thought made her
legs. *Have his way with her.*

A stupid, archaic phrase that sent even stupider, more
archaic pulses down her body. So they'd had an awkward
moment.

She rolled her eyes at the understatement. A *really*
awkward moment. And so what if she'd seen a lusty side
of a man she found attractive? Okay, gorgeous. All right,
hot as sin.

She was still a top-notch administrative assistant who
knew beyond a shadow of a doubt that office affairs were
for fools who liked to job hop. And he was a very important, busy man who had an electronic black book with
the name and private cell phone number of every available model, debutante and businesswoman in Miami-
Dade County.

She was still an employee, and he was still the boss.
Period. End of fantasy.

She tapped on his door, opening it as she did. She'd
always done that, but this morning, the intrusion felt more
intimate. He stood at the window, the cordless phone held
to his ear, his attention on the postcard view of Biscayne
Bay. Through a floor-to-ceiling window, sunlight glinted
off blue-violet waves, polka-dotted with pleasure craft and
cruise ships, fringed by emerald palm trees and the pastel
high-rises of Miami Beach on the horizon.

But the real view was inside and, as always, Anna
stole an eyeful.

Parker had removed his jacket, revealing the tailored cut
of a snow-white zillion-thread-count designer shirt pulled just
taut enough to hint at the toned, developed muscles under-

neath. The shirt was tucked neatly into dark trousers, custom-made to fit like a dream over one drool-inducing backside.

The man was a *god.*

He turned from the window and she averted her eyes before getting caught worshipping at the altar of his back-side.

"Can the legal crap, Brandon," he said into the phone, sliding one of his hands through closely cropped, thick black hair. "I don't care what the DNA test results will say. Can we or can we not contest this will?"

DNA? Contest the will? Anna frowned, but Parker just nodded to one of the guest chairs in front of his desk, issuing an unspoken invitation for her to sit. As always, he seemed utterly calm, the aura of authority that shimmered around him neatly in place. But there was something different in that clipped voice, and in the tense way he held his broad shoulders. His control was tied on with a tenuous thread today.

"Fine, you do that," he said, leaning his head to one side to work out a crick. "In the meantime, it's business as usual. *My* business." He glanced at Anna, who made a show of flipping her planner to the next clean page so she didn't stare. Even though she'd become quite adept at avoiding detection.

"Oh, damn it all, I completely forgot." His tone changed with the admission, and she instantly sat up, prepared to help him remember what he forgot. That was, after all, her job. Not ogling his perfectly shaped butt, impossibly wide shoulders or Adonis-like chest. Parker-gazing was just a side benefit.

"I can't go," he said to Brandon, sliding into the high-backed desk chair and reaching for his little black digital device and pressing a few buttons. "But, with the bomb you just dropped at this morning's reading, I think I need to be there more than ever."

He paused and Anna tried to psych out what he was talking about.

"But I'm way too swamped to consider going that far away," he added, "unless I charter a jet."

Of course. London.

"I have a ton of work to do this weekend," he continued, "and it's impossible to get anything done on a commercial flight."

Anna slipped a creamy-white card embossed with silver letters from the "pending" section of his calendar. Her fingers glided over the imprint of the International Hotel and Restaurant Association seal, over the gilded script inviting him to the annual ball at Guildhall in London. She'd been meaning to get a response from him so she could RSVP.

He chuckled softly, fiddling with the buttons on the PDA as he tucked the phone into one of those impressive shoulders.

"Yes. A date," he said casually to Brandon, and shot a lazy wink at Anna, which sent an involuntary stutter to her heart. "I suppose I'd need to get one of those, too."

Which of the lucky ladies would win that lottery?

Maxine, whose daddy owned half of Palm Beach? Or the nine-foot glamazon who'd been on the cover of *Vogue* twice? He'd been seeing a lot of her in the past few weeks. Maybe he'd go for that spunky redhead who owned the PR agency that had done some work for Garrison, Inc. last month. Sparks were certainly crackling in the conference room when that one came in for a meeting.

"As a matter of fact, I might have the perfect person." His gaze landed right on her, intense, relentless and unwavering. Exactly the way it had been when he'd devoured her with it in the bathroom.

A low, slow flame curled up her belly and started a familiar bonfire. One she'd become very good at dousing with four simple words that have saved legions of love-struck secretaries: *He's your boss, dummy.*

Suddenly, he stood, turned to the window and copped the voice he used to end a conversation instantly. "Keep me posted, Brandon. And I'll let you know what I decide."

For a moment, he didn't move, but stared at the cloud-less blue sky, his back rising and falling with steady, slow breaths.

Then he turned and trained his midnight gaze on her. "As you can tell, Anna, I didn't get good news this morning."

She set the call sheet on his desk. "That must explain the seventeen voice-mail messages."

He scanned the list, and swore so softly she almost didn't hear it. "Brandon's right."

"About?"

"I have to be at the IH & RA ball in London. It's more important than ever that I maintain…" He paused, assessing her as though he was wondering just how much to tell her. "Leadership."

"Your leadership is never in doubt."

He tilted his head, acknowledging the compliment with shuttered lids that said he believed the opposite. At least, at the moment. Then he yanked out his chair and sat, leaning forward the way he always did when he made a decision that he would not second-guess. Not that he'd ever second-guessed anything, ever, in his life.

"Please arrange for the charter jet company to have a Gulfstream V ready to leave tomorrow, very early, from Kendall-Tamiami Executive Airport. That will put me in London Friday evening, with plenty of time to make the function on Saturday and return on Sunday morning. I'll be back in the office on Monday. I'll need the Berkeley Suite at the Ritz-Carlton London. Don't let them tell you it's not available—"

"I'll use your name."

"Yes, and I'll need a limo to and from the event, which is—"

"At Guildhall."

"Right. And I have a driver in London I prefer—"

"Mr. Sanderson with the London Car Company."

He laughed softly. "Yes."

She scribbled the onslaught of instructions. "You'll want some files for the plane," she said.

"Of course."

"The financials on the Grand are up for review next week," she reminded him, still writing. "And you'll need the latest investment results, and the agenda for the exec committee meeting next—"

"Get me everything we have on the Garrison Grand-Bahamas."

She did look up at that, it threw her so completely. "The hotel in Nassau?"

"Everything," he repeated.

"Of course." She scratched another note, swallowing the question of *why?* A good admin didn't ask. "And you'll probably need to review your speech for the business council so I'll include the notes, and you have an appointment with a marketing firm regarding new collateral materials late next week, so no doubt you'll want a complete..." A strange tingling sensation suddenly froze her pen in hand. Slowly, she looked up from her pad to find him staring at her. "You do still want to meet with that firm on Thursday afternoon, right?"

Staring? No. Bottomless brown bedroom eyes practically swallowed her whole.

"What's the matter?" she asked, striking a neutral chord in her voice despite the way her limbs turned heavy.

"Make it easy on me, Anna, and come to London."

Oh. *Oh.* "Make what easy?"

"The *work*. You know so much about my work and you're so incredible…incredibly organized. I can only rationalize this much time away from the office if I'm productive. And with you, I'm productive."

The work. Of course. Why else would he want her to go to London? And why else would she even consider it?

"You can have comp vacation days to make up for the lost weekend," he added, as though she were actually worried about that. He had no way of knowing that her hesitation had nothing to do with losing a weekend, and everything to do with losing her mind. Proximity to the object of her steamiest nightly fantasies could drive her crazy.

"That's no problem," she said slowly. "I don't mind working the weekend."

"Then you'll go." He smiled, a genuine grin that he saved for when he won a small victory in business. Something he did about a million times a day. "Perfect. You'll need something very formal. That ball at Guildhall is over the top."

"The *ball?*" He couldn't be serious. "You want *me* to go to the ball?"

He laughed lightly. "That's the idea, Cinderella. Why would I dig up a date when you'll already be there?"

Like he'd have to dig far. "Because…" She couldn't think of a reason. Except that one.

He's your boss, dummy.

Unless what he'd seen in the bathroom made him think of her differently.

"Mr. Garrison, uh, Parker," she said, standing just so she could gain the minor advantage of height for once. "I'm sorry about this morning. I—"

He pointed toward the bathroom door. "That?" He waved away her concern as if it were no more than a flea. "Totally forgotten, I assure you." Tapping the call sheet, he added, "Better get that charter booked and get all the files in order, and I'll get to these seventeen calls."

Done. Decision made. No arguing or second-guessing or trying to explain that she couldn't, wouldn't, shouldn't go to London with him. Because she could, and she would.

Leaving his office, Anna found Sheila McKay in the act of depositing more handwritten messages.

"These came to the front desk while you were in with Mr. Garrison," the receptionist said. "The phones absolutely haven't stopped since that meeting ended."

"I just gave him seventeen others," Anna said with a sigh. "Looks like it's going to be a busy day."

Sheila wrinkled a picture-perfect nose, which fit her picture-perfect face and body. Anna hadn't been surprised to learn the stunning woman was a former Playmate who'd probably filled her bunny suit very nicely. She'd always been very friendly with Anna, especially since Anna had received the promotion to work for the CEO. But Anna remained distant with all her coworkers.

Friends wanted to know your past.

"So," Sheila said, sliding a well-toned hip on the corner of Anna's desk. "What went down in Garrison land? Did the old man drop a bomb from the grave or something?"

The words *DNA test* and *contest the will* rang in Anna's ears.

"I wouldn't know," she said coolly. Even if she did, she wouldn't tell the receptionist.

"There's buzz, you know," Sheila whispered, undaunted. "Mario in the mail room told me La Grande Madame left the conference room muttering obscenities, and is rumored to have had a bottle open before the limo door closed."

No wonder Mario had been in the mailroom since the day John Garrison had started the company. Gossips didn't get promoted. Anna flipped through the messages, deciding the best way to deflect the conversation.

"I'm really in the weeds, Sheila, trying to get Mr. Garrison ready for a trip to London."

Sheila levered off the desk with a sigh of resignation. "London, huh? Ah, the lucky lifestyles of the rich and famous. Must be nice." With a wave, she disappeared around the corner and left Anna with her mountain of messages.

Was it nice? She was about to find out. She knew she should be honored, excited and delighted for the opportunity to spend a weekend working in London.

But she had so much to hide, starting with the fact that she had a killer crush on her boss. But, honestly, that was the least of her secrets. And, if she wasn't careful, Parker Garrison could find out something far worse than the fact that he was the object of a few daydreams.

And that would be a nightmare.

Two

"We've reached our cruising altitude, Mr. Garrison. Would you care for the usual?" The lone flight attendant on the G5 that the Garrison family routinely rented for business travel smiled benevolently at him. Her prematurely gray hair was, as always, pulled back into an elegant bun, her simple dark suit unmarred by even a fleck of lint.

"Thank you, Christine, I would. Anna?"

Across the small expanse that separated the two widest leather recliners on the plane, Anna had already lined a granite-topped table with a sea of manila folders and papers, and she had a laptop open and fired up for work.

"It depends," she said. "What is the usual?"

"Tomato juice and Tabasco."

She made a face. "Coffee, please."

"Come on, Anna," he urged. "Live dangerously."

He hoped for a clever quip, an easy smile, but got only a shake of her head.

"Just coffee, thank you." When the attendant nodded and moved toward the galley, Anna lifted a paper and held it toward him. "I've compiled a list of pending open items for your attention, Mr. Garrison."

He didn't remind her to call him Parker. Anna Cross was back to business in a big way. It was as though she'd been wearing a sign that said This Is Work, Not Fun ever since she'd arrived at the executive airport and climbed out of her little Saturn wearing her most staid suit selected from a wardrobe that couldn't be called anything but *ultraconservative*. Navy jacket, shapeless trousers, flat shoes.

Where was the girl who felt pretty in pink underwear?

Parker took the list, and reminded himself that he was the one who'd suggested she accompany him to *work*. He'd made that clear. At least, that was how he rationalized what was, at the moment, an impulsive idea brought on by the not-so-semi state of arousal the bathroom encounter had left him in.

He knew why he'd suggested Anna accompany him to London.

But did she? Sure, she was a terrific, grade-A, indispensable administrative assistant. Sure, she was attractive, classy and intelligent enough to make small talk with the high rollers at the hotel gala. And best of all, he trusted her. She had no gold digger's interest in his money, ready to translate one weekend in Europe into a lifetime of luxury like so many of the women he knew.

But, to be honest, not one of those was the real reason he'd made the unorthodox suggestion. The real reason was simple: he liked what he'd seen in that bathroom. And he wanted to see more. And seeing, he knew as sure as he breathed, wouldn't be enough.

Under any other circumstances, he'd make his move and he'd make it in about five minutes, launching a romantic, sex-charged weekend with champagne and hot kisses at thirty thousand feet. Seducing a woman was an art and a pleasure he took seriously. And often.

But something indefinable held him back. Something oddly unfamiliar had him waiting for a clear invitation, a straightforward cue from her.

Maybe she'd take off her jacket, playfully taste his spicy tomato juice, unclip her barrette and give her hair a sensual shake. That was what other women would do. They'd throw in a head-tilting giggle; slide their bare, pedicured feet on his lap and let the games begin.

But not Anna.

She pulled a pair of butt-ugly reading glasses out of her purse and slipped them up her pert nose. She tightened the clip that held her hair severely off a face devoid of anything but lip gloss and maybe mascara. Then she took her copy of his agenda, pointed to item number one, cleared her throat and said, "You mentioned the Nassau property. I have the files."

Not only did she refuse to send a single cue of feminine interest, she doused his low simmer by mentioning the biggest headache in his life.

He took the file and flipped it open.

"Is there something in particular you're looking for?" she asked.

There sure was. Dirt. Problems. Issues. Anything that could get rid of the half sister who'd just been named his equal partner at Garrison, Inc. "Just want to see how the business is doing."

"Last quarter's financials are on the left side, including occupancy rates and banquet revenue," she told him. "On the right, you'll see information about new resort programs and key employee files. The manager of the resort, Cassie Sinclair, seems to be running things quite smoothly."

At the mention of her name, Parker sucked in a slow and disgusted breath. He flipped through the pages, immaculately ordered and filed, frowning at the excellent revenue stream and the strong outlook for the next season based on advance reservations.

"Is something wrong?"

Yes, something was very, very wrong. He wanted the property to be a disaster. Wanted something he could hang on Cassie Sinclair to prove she couldn't be a Garrison.

"No," he assured her.

"Oh, I thought I might have misfiled something."

"Have you ever misfiled anything, Anna?" he asked with a teasing smile.

A soft blush rose in her cheeks. "If you're asking if I ever make mistakes, I think you, of all people, know that I do."

Mistakes like lingering in his shower a little too long? He held her gaze, still hoping for a spark of connection, but she looked away—as she always did—just as Christine returned with the drinks, some fruit and freshly baked muffins.

Parker returned his attention to the file. "The place is turning a nice profit," he said, half to himself.

"You make it sound like that's a problem."

Should he confide in his assistant? Maybe a little shared confidence would loosen her up. At least get her to slide out of that straitjacket she wore. Plus, he needed someone to talk to. Someone he trusted.

He lifted his tomato juice and took a long drink before he dove in. "Cassie Sinclair, it seems, is more than just the manager of the Garrison Grand-Bahamas."

"She is?"

"She's my half sister."

Anna's jaw dropped an inch. "No way."

He gave her a bittersweet smile. "Evidently there is a way. It's called an affair and my father had one for a long time, resulting in the birth of a woman who is now, according to his will, my equal partner in Garrison, Inc. and—" he held the file up "—the owner of this hotel."

"I don't believe it," she said, dropping back into her seat.

"Neither do I. But that's why God invented lawyers," he said with a shrug. "And why I have to make an appearance in London this weekend."

"Will she be there?"

"Oh, I doubt it. But it's only a matter of time until this gets out to the very small and incestuous hospitality industry. It can't help my business. I'm attending this event for visibility and positioning. More of a PR move than one that will impact the bottom line."

"So that's why you were talking about DNA testing and contesting the will," she said. "Oh, and why...your mother..." Her voice drifted off.

So the rumor mill had already started churning.

"My mother has her way of coping." He picked up the drink again. "And I'm afraid it's not Tabasco in her tomato juice."

She gave him a sympathetic look. "Your family is strong. You'll weather this storm."

"I hope you're right."

"You just have to stay focused and keep running everything the way you have. You can't let this distract you."

The unsolicited—and amazingly accurate—advice took him by surprise. "You're right, Anna. Very astute." He smiled and leaned forward, inexplicably drawn to her. "Thank you for being so understanding."

She held his gaze just long enough to give him hope that the cue he wanted was right around the corner. But she just handed him another file.

"When you're ready to go over the agenda for the marketing-firm meeting, it's all in here. And I'm able to take any e-mail dictation now," she added, tapping the open laptop. "I'll download it and send it when we arrive in London."

Oh, yeah. Anna Cross was all business today, and being a smart CEO, he ignored the urge to reach across the space that separated them and unclip her hair just to see what she'd do. She was way too valuable an asset to him to let hormones screw it up.

So he took the cue—even if it wasn't the one he wanted—along with the file, and worked for a solid nine hours, through breakfast, lunch and almost no small talk, until they landed.

Through it all, she never tired, never complained and never even took the damn jacket off. Maybe that was the real reason he didn't make the move to seduce her: they were kindred spirits. Workaholics, both of them, with a bone-deep love for control over their respective worlds.

Sex, in fact, could really screw that up.

By the time they landed and took a late-night cab ride through the still-vibrating streets of London, Parker was entirely comfortable with keeping the weekend on the level of strictly business. He abandoned the idea of taking her sightseeing the next day; they—or at least, he—would work, grilling Brandon Washington on the situation in the Bahamas and tracking the progress of several high-power land deals he had in the works.

Tomorrow night, he would introduce Anna as his assistant and she would no doubt wear her hair in a bun, don a conservative dress and stay stone-cold sober.

"Wow!" Anna froze midstep as they followed the cheerful old doorman into the smothering luxury that was the Ritz-Carlton London.

"Yeah, it's not exactly the Miami Beach hip of the Garrison Grand," Parker agreed. "This is pure old-world sophistication. You either like it or you feel suffocated. I, personally, love it."

"It's fantastic," she said, her voice a little hushed as she took in the three-story rotunda that capped the lobby, trimmed by ornate gilded woodwork.

Smiling at her enthusiasm, he stepped away to check in. But after a few keystrokes and frowns, the formally dressed clerk informed Parker that there'd been an error in the system and Ms. Cross's room was not available.

"Not ready or not available?" Parker asked.

"We are so very, deeply sorry, Mr. Garrison," the solicitous clerk, who obviously had not been in the hotel business long enough to recognize Parker's last name, crooned softly. "We are booked, overbooked and double booked with several very large events this weekend."

Parker knew, without the slightest doubt, that a single word with a manager would get a room. He'd been raised in this business and "no rooms" meant there were a half dozen on reserve.

"Your suite has three bedrooms, Mr. Garrison, and it's quite lovely and spacious," the clerk added. "And perhaps something will become available tomorrow."

Parker squeezed the bridge of his nose, fighting the exhaustion that came with trans-Atlantic travel. He turned to see Anna, who still scanned the lobby with a little bit of wonder in her eyes. There really was plenty of room in that suite. She'd love the decor.

And if it got a little cozy...

He nodded to the clerk. "We'll make due with that, then."

After a moment, a bellman whisked their luggage ahead and Parker joined Anna with a regretful smile. "Slight change in plans," he said.

"Oh?"

"There's no room for you."

She drew back, frowning. "I know I booked it. And, surely, if you tell them who—"

He held up a hand in agreement. "I can fight it, absolutely. But the suite has three bedrooms, all with their own baths, and enough room for a party of fifty people." He grinned. "I believe I had one there once."

She shrugged, a little weariness—or was it wariness?—giving a delicate set to her jaw. "All right. I'm beat, anyway. I just need a shower and sleep."

He tilted his head and put a casual hand on her shoulder to guide her through the lobby. "I only have one rule."

She slowed her step. "Which is?"

"No singing in the shower."

Late the next afternoon, Anna broke the rule.

Secretly, quietly and probably way off-key, she warbled a pathetic version of "Can't Help Loving That Man" from *Showboat* as she let blistering hot water pulse over her skin.

She *couldn't* help it. Showers were made for singing.

Anyway, Parker hadn't emerged from the wood-paneled library long enough to even enjoy the ridiculous opulence of a suite that was about three times the size of Anna's little house in Coral Gables, let alone hear her in the shower. And, oh, what he'd missed while he mumbled and barked orders to his lawyer, his accountant, his minions.

Anna could have spent the day just roaming the endless array of museum-quality rooms, admiring the Louis-the-something furniture, taking in the view of the avenues and stores from every arched window. As it was, she'd lost half an hour that morning just brushing her fingers over silk, damask and velvet pillows of celery and sage on delicate settees and graceful dining-room chairs.

But like always, the best view in the place was the one of her boss, wearing casual khaki pants and a simple but achingly expensive pullover and, God help her, no shoes.

That had been what finally sent her into the streets of London. Not his suggestion that she use the car and driver to explore. Not his implication that he needed complete privacy to conduct his business. No, what sent her out to the shops of Piccadilly, past Buckingham Palace and into the pristine paths of Hyde Park were Parker Garrison's bare feet.

She closed her eyes and paused midsong, water sluicing over her bare skin, as hot as the fire that tightened her stomach into a knot of arousal. She thought she'd seen everything attractive on the man...but she'd never seen such beautiful feet.

Long and narrow, strong boned with the faintest dusting of black hairs on his toes and a high arch where his khaki pants broke.

Oh, Anna Cross, girl, you have it bad. Swooning over feet.

But she'd nearly dumped her china coffee cup when he'd emerged from his room that morning, the shoulders of his red shirt spotted from droplets of just-showered hair, the natural scent of his soap still clinging to him. Averting her gaze from his freshly shaven face, she'd looked down.

Big mistake.

When she'd returned to the suite only an hour ago, he'd still been in the damn library, with the door closed. So she'd decided to start getting ready for the gala, planning to take a lot of time and care with her hair and makeup. After all, he'd said this was a PR move. It would be a PR disaster to arrive with a sad-looking date.

Getting ready might take some time because it had been many years since she'd arrived at a formal affair on the arm of a rich and powerful man. With a hard jerk, she twisted the knobs of the shower, wishing she could shut off the flow of her thoughts as easily. She didn't want to think about the man who'd changed everything. Not her boss, in that case, but her boss's rival.

But ever since she'd taken the job for Parker, thoughts of Michael Montgomery, another powerful, influential man, were close to the surface. The fact that once before she'd given in to a weakness for a handsome power broker with class, humor and style was nothing to be ashamed of, she reminded herself as she applied some makeup and twirled her hair into a French twist.

But her weakness had made her a pawn caught in the cross fire, forced to run and give up her home…all because she'd given in to an attraction to a man who was, ironically, very much like Parker Garrison.

Her father, a very wise man, had once told her that the definition of *fool* was someone who didn't learn from a mistake. She wasn't a fool. Was she?

When she'd been with Michael Montgomery, she'd been twenty-four, young and naive. Now she was nearly twenty-nine, and had successfully escaped her past. Sure, she had a crush on Parker the size of the Garrison Grand, but she was human and female. And she'd managed her attraction for three months.

But now, she was in London, sharing a suite with him, no less. And about to slip into a slinky gown she hadn't worn for four years. And no doubt she'd have to dance with him.

Oh, how much could a girl take before she did something…foolish?

Makeup and hair done, she covered her skin with a lightly scented cream, stepped into tiny bikini panties and opened the closet door to inch the drab navy suit to the side.

He hadn't given her time to shop for something new, she thought as she touched the red silk. And she'd only worn this dress once, so it didn't make any sense to spend money on something else. Plus…oh, forget rationalizing. She loved the dress.

Fingering the plunging neckline, she remembered how beautiful she'd felt the last time she'd worn it—right before her boyfriend had betrayed her, and she'd been run out of Indiana by bad press and false accusations.

She buried the thought. Tonight, she'd just revel in the dress, in the thigh-revealing cut and the backless dip that nearly touched her tailbone and the flared skirt that shimmered like liquid fire when she walked.

Anna reached for the hanger, a little sad she'd cover the revealing bodice and back with a simple black pashmina wrap and take small steps so as not to show too much leg. Because, all rationalization aside, she didn't need to attract any attention.

And she had to remember that powerful, sexy, controlling men with smoldering smiles and mouthwatering bodies were dangerous. Especially, oh, God, especially if one of the things they controlled was your paycheck.

She slipped on the dress, fastened the halter top and added some simple silver earrings and strappy black sandals. She dropped a tube of lipstick and a compact into her evening bag. Now where had she put the wrap?

"Anna?" From the sound of Parker's voice, he was outside her door. "The limo's here."

"I'll be right out," she promised, flipping through the closet for the pashmina. Then two drawers. Then her empty suitcase.

Was it possible the woman who never forgot anything had left the cover-up at home? She closed her eyes and pictured it hanging over the chair in her bedroom where she'd placed it with a mental note to pack it last.

"Damn." She'd forgotten to pack it at all.

"Anna? Do you need help with a zipper or something?"

Or something. She fingered the plunging neckline and swiped her hand over the curve of her hip. Evidently she wasn't going to be able to hide a thing from anyone tonight.

She put her hand on the doorknob and took a deep breath. "I seem to have forgotten my wrap," she said. "I hope that's not a problem."

When she opened the door, she inhaled sharply at the sight of Parker in a tuxedo. Really, there ought to be a law against looking like that.

He merely stepped back, and made absolutely no effort to hide the slow sweep of his gaze over her face and body. "Uh, no." His voice was tight, the way it had been in the bathroom the other morning, and his eyes turned just as dark and hungry. "That is definitely not a problem."

But the way he reached for her hand, and the way that designer tux rested on his broad shoulders, and the way he smelled like cinnamon and spice...oh, that was a problem.

He leaned a little too close and took a deep breath, a soft moan in his chest. "You certainly are good at hiding...things."

She managed a tight smile. "Not really."

Oh, yes. The problems were just starting to mount.

Three

"I thought I should wear a wrap."

Parker gave in to the urge to check her out top to bottom one more time. Anna was stunning. Extraordinary. Perfect.

"*Why* would you cover that up?" he asked.

"I just… I'm cold." She rubbed her bare arms self-consciously, the gesture drawing her breasts together in the most provocative way.

He'd reached to touch her shoulder, but his hand continued over her back, drawing her closer, warming her. "You don't need a wrap. You've got a date."

Goose bumps rose on her skin, and beneath the thin red material that hugged her breasts, her nipples hardened, sending a few gallons of his blood below the belt.

What was that stupid decision he'd made on the plane? Something about kindred spirits and messing things up with sex and…

Never mind. Some decisions just screamed to be second-guessed.

"You look incredible," he said, letting genuine admiration warm his voice as he leaned closer and took a whiff of her musky perfume. "And you smell like heaven."

"Thanks," she said softly, stepping away from him in one easy move. "You clean up nice, too, Mr.—"

He pointed a playful finger at her. "Don't you dare."

"Parker." She smiled and moved another step away. "I'm sorry, it's a hard habit to break."

"I'll help you." Reaching for her hand, he lifted her knuckles to his mouth and placed a soft kiss on her silky skin. "Every time you use the word *mister,* I'm going to kiss you."

Her eyelashes shuttered and the goose bumps returned, but she laughed softly. "Kind of like Pavlov's dog?"

"Nothing like Pavlov's dog." He guided her toward the door. "But consider yourself warned. And every time you force me to kiss you, it's going to get…" He tempered his smoky look with a half smile. "More serious."

Maybe that would nudge her toward that "cue" he'd been waiting for.

"Then I'll have to be very careful of what I say," she promised, her pretty mouth turned up in a teasing smile.

As they walked toward the elevator, he drank in her staggering combination of sexuality and elegance. The gown narrowed at her waist, then flared and then…

Oh, man. The thigh-high slit made his mouth go bone dry. How was a guy supposed to keep his hands out of that treasure trove?

He hit the elevator call button and leaned closer to her. "I have to tell you," he said, glancing down at the open pleat. "You have great legs, Anna."

Color darkened her cheeks. "Thank you, Mist—"

Parker grinned as he dipped down and kissed her cheek. "What were you going to say?"

She chuckled softly. "Thank you, Parker."

"My pleasure," he said, his voice rich with double meaning. Sliding his arm around her waist, he placed his mouth close to her ear as the elevator bell dinged and the doors opened. "Next time it'll be on the lips."

"Well, if it isn't the Grand Garrison himself."

Parker froze at the ice in the familiar voice, the frisson of sexual play extinguished by the sound of an archenemy. He led Anna into the car, sparing Jordan Jefferies no more than a passing glance as he nodded hello. Just long enough to see the tall, muscular man looked tan and fit, and wore a tuxedo.

Parker swore mentally. Jefferies was headed to the same gala, no doubt.

"I'm afraid your escort is too rude to introduce us," Jordan said to Anna. "I'm Jordan Jefferies."

She gave the man a blank look as if she'd never even heard of him before. But how could she not? She must have heard the name around the office. She had to know the Jefferies brothers, both this one and the adopted Emilio, were the bane of Parker's existence. What the hell was he doing here, anyway? He hadn't been on the guest list Parker had requested to see before he'd left.

"Anna Cross," she said politely, shaking his hand.

Jefferies turned her fingers, gave a little fake Euro-bow and kissed her knuckles. Parker seethed silently.

"A pleasure, Anna," Jefferies said.

"Couldn't find a date, Jefferies?" Parker said, only half teasing.

"I decided to fly over at the last minute," he replied, his blue eyes riveted on Anna. "And certainly I couldn't find anyone to rival this beautiful woman."

Anna sneaked a sideways glance of disbelief at Parker, and he wanted to kiss her again for not succumbing to the wiles of this snake. Instead, he slid a possessive arm around her and eased her into his side. Where she'd be spending the evening.

And, if all went well, the night.

The car stopped at a lower floor and when the doors opened, Parker's stomach dropped at the sight of yet another archenemy.

Emilio Jefferies nodded to his brother, but his sage-green eyes swept over Parker, his olive complexion darkening just a little. "Parker. Pleasant surprise to see you here."

Parker doubted that it was pleasant *or* a surprise, but he did the right thing and introduced the other Jefferies brother to Anna.

"I assume you are both headed to the gala," Anna said.

"We are," Emilio acknowledged.

"I'm sure you'll have a wonderful time," she said.

He nodded and looked at Parker. "How is your family?"

"Fine." Parker studied the numbers above the door, calculating just how many more seconds he'd have to exchange oxygen with Jordan and Emilio Jefferies.

"Your sisters?" Jordan asked.

Parker speared him with a look. He'd kill either of his sisters if they even talked to these two snakes. "Fine," he repeated.

"Miss Cross." Jordan directed his attention back to Anna, ignoring Parker. "Are you in the hospitality industry as well?"

"Anna is my assistant," Parker said before she could answer, infusing the pride he felt into his voice.

Jefferies notched a knowing eyebrow. "Well, that must be convenient."

Parker's fingers twitched with the desire to land something *convenient* in Jordan Jefferies's smug face but Anna just relaxed into him, her smile all grace and class. "It certainly is, as Mr. Garrison is so gifted when it comes to mixing business and pleasure."

Jordan drew back as the door opened, surprise and admiration on his sculpted features. He stepped aside and let Anna out of the elevator first.

"You know I love nothing more than taking what you want, Garrison," Jordan murmured to Parker under his breath.

"And I love nothing more than making sure you don't."

"Then you'd better hold on to your assistant."

"I plan to."

"And everything else," Emilio added with a smile that looked more like a sneer.

Parker gave them both venomous looks, then muscled past to walk Anna through the Ritz lobby. They didn't speak until they'd been whisked through the doors and cocooned into a waiting limousine.

"That was the perfect way to handle them," Parker said as he handed her a bubbling glass of champagne the driver had just poured.

Anna accepted it, and tilted her head. "Why, thank you, Mr. Garrison."

She'd used the name on purpose, he had no doubt. Flashing her a victorious grin, he leaned closer and brushed her lips with his.

"Next time," he whispered against her lips, "it's a French kiss."

"Thanks for the warning." The crystal clinked. "Parker."

He sipped the champagne, admired his beautiful date and imagined just how many times he could get her to call him Mr. Garrison in the next few hours.

* * *

In no time at all, Anna surrendered.

How could she not? No woman could resist the magic of a magnificent, historic banquet hall shimmering with a million candles and a thousand elegantly dressed guests. She just gave in to the music, the moment and, of course, the man. The sounds of a full orchestra reverberated off the carved stone walls of Guildhall and echoed from the grandiose stained glass windows. Laughter, tinkling glasses and chatter vibrated around the well-dressed guests gliding across the glasslike marble floor.

From the moment they'd arrived, Parker teased, flirted, danced and introduced Anna as if she were his most prized treasure, keeping one possessive hand on the small of her back.

As they danced to a ballad, he whispered tidbits about the guests, making her laugh with his insights, impressing her with how well he knew so many of the people in his industry.

"That's Davis Brookheiser, the owner of that new line of spa resorts out in California," he said, tilting his head toward an older man who slowly—very slowly—waltzed with an attractive young woman.

"And that's Davis's daughter?" Anna asked, letting just a little sarcasm tinge her voice.

He laughed. "That would be the third Mrs. Brookheiser." Then he frowned a little at the couple. "Maybe the fourth. I've lost track of Davis's trophies."

As the couple danced by, Anna caught Mrs. Brookheiser staring at Parker over her much shorter husband's shoulder. But he ignored the obvious attention, keeping his focus on Anna.

"She hasn't lost track of you," Anna teased.

He applied a gentle amount of pressure to her back,

easing her closer so she could feel the steel muscles of his body and the unmistakable message of desire in his touch.

"No thanks. I've got my hands nicely full at the moment."

Blood rushed through her veins, firing up her nerve endings, making her boneless and light-headed. If he had any idea how many nights she'd put herself to sleep with this very scenario in her imagination. Parker, holding her and making promises with his eyes. Parker, inches from her mouth for a kiss.

Parker.

She took a slow, steadying breath and forced herself to admire the pageantry around her. She had to remember why she was dead set against acting on her attraction. She had to remember why he was all wrong for her.

He's your boss, dummy.

Yeah. Right. She was having a very difficult time remembering that. At the moment, she could barely remember her own name.

"Just imagine how many royals and prime ministers have danced on this very floor," she said, leaning away, striving for casual conversation even though the music and the movement were anything but casual.

But her gesture just gave him an opportunity to lower his gaze to her throat, study the V in her neckline and eventually return for a good, long examination of her mouth. Only then did he politely follow her glance around.

"Many, since Guildhall has been hosting high-end affairs since the fourteen hundreds."

"I guess the association can't hold this event at a hotel," she mused. "That would be like playing favorites."

"Exactly," he agreed. "This has to remain neutral ground for all the members. See that gray-haired matriarch under the arch? Genevieve Dufresne."

"The Swiss resort Dufresne?"

He gave her a satisfied smile. "You do pay attention to the business, don't you? Yes, she is the head of the mighty Dufresne family. So, believe me, there might be a spirit of shared camaraderie since we're all in similar businesses, but there's competition in the air."

"Like in the elevator."

He made a distasteful face.

"Why do you hate them so much?"

The music ended and he guided her toward the table, where she picked up her handbag.

"Let's walk outside," he suggested, pausing to snag two crystal champagne flutes when a white-tailed waiter walked by.

She took hers, but didn't sip. The atmosphere and company were intoxicating enough. They wandered through one of the dozens of soaring archways that led to various halls, a museum and crypts housing centuries of folklore, legends and art.

On a wide stone veranda, where a number of partygoers dallied at tables and benches to enjoy the evening air, they found a cozy bench, blocked by a large planter and secluded from the other people.

"Perfect," he said, taking her hand and tugging her next to him.

"You didn't answer my question," Anna said after a moment. "Why do you hate the Jefferies brothers?"

He gave her a wry smile. "You could ruin a perfectly awesome night with that line of questioning. Truthfully, I don't hate anyone, but if I were going to, Jordan and Emilio would head the list."

"Why?"

"They're ruthless, cutthroat empire builders."

She stifled a smile. "And you're not."

He opened his mouth to argue, but then let out a soft, self-deprecating laugh. "Not ruthless."

"Yes, ruthless."

"Not cutthroat."

"Yes, cutthroat."

"Not… All right." He grinned. "But not underhanded. And I think they are and I don't want that womanizer Jordan around my sisters." He inched closer and draped a possessive arm around her. "Or you."

"Me?" The champagne tickled her nose, mixed with the soft, masculine scent of man. Unable to resist, she nestled into the expensive fabric of his tuxedo jacket.

"Yes, you," he said, his face perilously close to hers.

"He would want nothing to do with me," she insisted.

"Not when you're doing your level best to hide your assets behind your shapeless suits. But the secret's out now." He brought his face closer to hers, and lowered his voice to barely above a whisper. "You are a beautiful, sexy woman, Anna."

She closed her eyes as the compliment washed over her, more potent than if she'd thrown back her champagne and his.

"Thank you," she said, searching for some way to divert the conversation to a less personal area. "So how do you know the Jefferies brothers are cutthroat and ruthless? I don't recall any dealings with them since I've worked for you."

"You sure know how to wreck a moment," he said, a smile on his lips. "Those brothers have made it no secret that they want to give Garrison, Inc. a run for its money. And they are doing a good job," he conceded, taking a swallow of champagne. "They've made some major inroads into the luxury hospitality and entertainment fields."

"You don't strike me as a man who worries about competition."

"Of course I do. I worry about squashing it. And I worry about the fate and status of the Garrison brand, which, as you know, I'm responsible for." A shadow crossed his expression. "At least I was until my father's will was read."

"What's happening to the brand?" Anna relaxed a little, encouraged that the conversation had been steered away from the undercurrent of sexual tension that had been ricocheting off the Guildhall walls for the last few hours.

"We're just taking hits in the media, and some investors I'd counted on have backed out from deals for no apparent reason. Properties I want have suddenly been sold to someone else." He snorted softly. "Usually to someone named Jefferies." After a moment, he added, "I seriously think there's a leak in my company."

A shiver danced down her spine. "A leak?"

"A spy. A mole. A...*someone* feeding inside information to competitors. To the Jefferieses." He turned to her, his expression fierce. "I'm going to find out who it is and ruin them."

White lights burst behind her eyes and it wasn't stars or romance blinding her. It was the hard, cold smack of her past hitting her in the face.

"A spy?" She heard the shakiness in her voice.

"Don't sound incredulous. It happens, you know."

Oh, she knew. She knew firsthand. She knew so well it hurt. "I've read about things like that." The only problem was that when she read about them, her name was in the articles.

Her name—not the man who'd committed the crime. Not Michael Montgomery, a man she'd thought she loved and trusted. A man who'd used her to get into the computer system of her boss, another CEO.

The night air suddenly seemed stifling and the back of her neck burned with perspiration. If Parker ever learned of her past, of the accusation—however wrong—that she'd let her lover access files from her boss's computer, then she would be fired. Of that, there was no doubt.

Who would ever give her a chance to explain? Her old boss hadn't. The media hadn't. She'd just had to run.

"All it would take is one person who has knowledge of my deals to slip the information to one of the Jefferieses," he continued, his voice suddenly sounding distant as blood thundered through her ears.

"Do you think…someone has?"

"I'm certain of it. Jordan and Emilio Jefferies weren't going to come to this gala. They weren't on the list. But then, wham. They show up and no one knew I was coming but a handful of Garrison employees."

Including *her.* At his words, her stomach tightened, her fingertips tingled, her head spun. Only this time, her reaction had nothing to do with attraction, but everything to do with the fear of detection.

Of course, she was innocent. Totally and completely and wholly innocent, and the charges against her had been dropped. But the stain was still there.

Could a man who'd just admitted he was ruthless, cut-throat and competitive even see past that stain? Could he ever see beyond the fact that she had let one other corporate rival into the inner workings of another CEO's desk…albeit unknowingly?

"It really bothers me," he said, still staring into the night.

She had to get the subject changed, fast.

"In fact," he continued, "I'm more determined than ever to find the leak."

She had to get him off course.

"And with the change in my father's—"

She reached up and pressed her lips to his cheek. He froze, then slowly turned toward her. "What are you doing, Miss Cross?"

"What do you think I'm doing, Mr. Garrison?"

He broke into a slow, sexy smile. "What did you call me?"

She lifted her face in invitation, forming the words she knew would derail his train of thought. "Mr. Garrison."

He closed his mouth over hers instantly, kissing her exactly the way he did everything…thoroughly, expertly, with masterful control and brilliant timing.

Parting her lips, she allowed his tongue to explore her mouth. Chills and heat warred over her skin as he glided his hands over her bare back, burrowing his fingers into the hair at the nape of her neck.

She tilted her head, and he deepened the kiss, a tender moan vibrating his chest. He pulled her closer and murmured her name against her mouth.

"Let's go back to the hotel," he whispered in the kiss. "Now."

Okay, she had definitely changed the direction of the conversation.

He stood, pulling her into him. "I want you," he told her, confirming that with a full-body press that left no doubt he was aroused.

She melted into the kiss, torn by a secret delight that she'd caused that hard ridge against her stomach, and the secret horror that he'd find out why.

She inched back, catching her breath. "Parker…I…"

"Unless you'd rather talk business some more," he said with a playful kiss on her nose.

"Not on your life," she said. And, God knows, she meant it.

Four

When Anna sent a signal, she made it crystal clear.

Somehow, Parker knew that would happen. He knew if he bided his time, easing her slowly into a comfortable, sensual, intimate place, she would give him the go-ahead to take that kiss he'd been thinking about all night.

He'd been fighting arousal since she'd opened the door—hell, since he'd found her in the bathroom the other day. Every dance made him want to touch more; every time she laughed or asked a question, leaned gently against him or just sent him a subtle look of pure lust, his jaw slackened for some mouth-to-mouth contact with hers.

He thought he'd imagined the occasional admiring glance in the past, but tonight, Anna's defenses were down. And her interest was up. Way up.

"The limo's right over there," he said, nudging her in that direction. "We don't need to stay a minute more."

A glimmer of uncertainty lit her eyes.

"Unless you want to," he said, placing one finger on her chin to turn her face to him. He trailed that finger down her throat, into the dip between her collarbones, and then lower, barely touching, barely skimming her flesh.

Her eyelids fluttered and her lips parted.

"It's entirely up to you," he added, dropping close to her ear to whisper the words and nibble her lobe.

She arched slightly with a quick breath. Then she closed her eyes and nodded so slightly, he almost missed it. With a firm hand on her back, he walked toward the waiting limo, and addressed the driver.

"We'll go directly to the Ritz, John," he said as he climbed in the car behind Anna. Although it might be fun to play in the limo while they tooled around London for an hour, he didn't want her in a car. He wanted to get her back to the suite and directly in his bed.

He would, however, have to keep her warm on the way back.

Settling in next to her, he offered champagne, but she declined. He touched a button and filled the car with the soft strains of Andrea Bocelli's new-millennium version of classical music and her eyes sparkled.

"I love this music."

"You love music, I noticed."

She smiled. "Broadway tunes are my favorite, actually."

"West Side Story?"

Even in the dim light of the car, he could see her flush. "I'm sorry about that, again."

"I'm not. Use the shower in there whenever you like. Leave the door open." He curled an arm around her and feathered her hair with a kiss. "I liked the view."

"But not the song."

He laughed and moved his mouth to lightly kiss her cheek. "Your heart was into it, that's all that matters to me."

She turned to him, her face suddenly very serious, the laughter gone from her eyes. "My heart's into everything that I do," she assured him. "Even my work."

"Good," he murmured, inching closer to her mouth, not thinking too hard about the sincerity in her eyes. His mind was not on work at the moment. "I like that in a woman."

He kissed her again, working to keep it light and easy, but hot and hard was winning the battle. He tunneled his fingers into her hair and found the comb that held it in place. In one twist of his wrist, her hair tumbled.

He finger-combed it, inhaling the sweet fragrance, gliding his tongue over her teeth. She leaned her head back against the seat so he could kiss the tender skin of her throat and nibble his way into the V of her dress.

She tasted sweet and hot and smooth.

Unable to stop himself, he slid one hand from her nape, down the halter strap to the tender, precious curve of her breast, covering her easily. Instantly, her nipple pebbled against his palm, firing a blast of lava-hot blood through him, pulling groans of pleasure from both their throats.

"Parker." She sighed, lifting herself just enough to let him know she enjoyed the touch.

"Glad we're back on a first-name basis," he teased, dragging his hand along the tight fit of her waist, over her hip and finding the slit that had called to him all night.

His hand hit flesh and her whole body shivered. He chuckled softly into another kiss. "Look what I found," he whispered, tracing the tight thigh with one fingertip, inching higher to torture both of them.

Another moan of delight shuddered through her. He quieted that with a long, wet, hungry kiss, opening his hand to caress the taut muscle of her thigh. His fingers moved higher, over velvety skin, anxious just to touch her once. Just to feel how creamy she was. Expertly, he ran his thumb once over the silky nub of her panties, eliciting a soft gasp in their kiss.

"Maybe we should take the long way back," he suggested, taking one more featherlight stroke over the damp silk between her legs.

Slowly, easily, she closed her fingers over his wrist and slid his hand away.

"Too fast?" he asked. "Too much? Too soon?"

The fire in her eyes said no to all of the above, but she nodded.

He took a deep breath and gave her a reassuring smile, placing his hand on a far less controversial spot on her waist. "I'll wait." He could. His body hummed with need, hard and relentless, but he would wait. "At least until we walk in the door."

She smiled, then caught her lower lip under her two front teeth with a heartbreakingly unsure expression.

"What's the matter?" he asked, cupping her jaw and lifting her face to meet his. "You're not sure? Are you…I mean, you've done this before, right?"

"I had a serious boyfriend when I lived in Indiana." Her whole expression changed with the admission.

He wasn't at all sure he wanted to hear about this boyfriend, at least not at this particular moment. But she obviously wanted to tell him something.

"What happened?" he asked.

She lowered her head, gnawed on that lip again, thinking. "He hurt me. He…"

A natural male fury whipped through him. "He forced you?"

"No, no," she said. "Nothing like that. He just…lied to me. He used me and I…" She sighed and turned to the window. "It cost me my job."

Oh. Suddenly her hesitation was totally understandable. She must have worked for the guy, and this would feel like history repeating itself. And what could he say?

"And you're worried that could happen again," he said.

"Can you, in good conscience, promise me that if I sleep with you, it would never affect my job?"

He breathed slowly, studying her. "I can't promise that, Anna." As much as his hardened, aroused body wanted him to make all sorts of promises, he couldn't actually make that one. Because it might change things in the office. That was life.

The limo slowed in front of the Ritz, and he gave her a moment to smooth her hair. When John opened the back door on her side, Parker watched her climb gracefully out of the car, the sexy red dress clinging to every curve he wanted to explore with his hands and mouth.

Nothing was going to happen to *his* career if they had sex and things didn't work out. He was smart enough to know that. And so was she.

He cleared his throat and willed his arousal to subside as they made their way to the elevator. When the doors closed he turned to her.

"Anna," he said, wrapping the hand that still held hers around her back. "You know what I want. But, it's your call." He resisted the urge to kiss her, but continued. "If that means we end up in bed together, well—" he smiled and touched her jaw with his other hand "—great. But…"

If it meant kissing her chastely good-night and keeping the best administrative assistant he ever had, that was great, too. Not *as* great, but Parker knew when to compromise and when to push.

The doors opened and he took her hand, leading her into the hushed hallway. He pulled out the room key and opened the massive double doors to the darkened suite, the only sound the steady thump of his heart while he waited for her decision.

He'd forgotten to leave a light on, and they stood in the shadows, inches apart. She hadn't spoken since they'd left the limo and he knew the next word she said would seal their fate.

She turned to him and slid her arms around his shoulders, locking at his neck. He resisted a grin of victory, but lowered his head for the kiss he expected.

"Thank you for the most amazing party I've ever been to." She rose on her toes, kissed his cheek and backed away. "Good night, Parker."

He could barely see her disappear into her room, but in the silence, he heard the lock turn. He stood in the dark for a few minutes, tapping the card key against his palm. The card key that she obviously didn't realize was a master and could open her bedroom door.

Smothering a soft sigh, he shook his head, the disappointment finally making it down to the lower half of his body to deliver the bad news.

The lady said no.

He shimmied out of the tuxedo jacket, threw it over a delicate French provincial chair and strode to the bar, flipping over a brandy snifter and filling it with a solid slug of the good stuff. With one hand, he loosened his bow tie and unbuttoned the first two buttons of the tux shirt.

He took the drink to the balcony that ran the length of the salon, folding into a comfortable chair and inhaling the sounds and scents of an active avenue two stories below.

Didn't this beat all? He was in London, in his favorite suite, with a smoldering hot woman undressing in the next room...and he would be going to bed alone.

Why hadn't he thought this through when he'd issued the impulsive invitation? Because he'd been seeing legs in heels and hearing off-key songs in his head, that was why.

Drinking a little deeper than the heavy brandy called for, his throat burned. Hell, everything burned. He wanted her. He really wanted her.

But she wanted...

Now there was an unanswered question. What did Anna want? A promotion? A boyfriend? A husband? A good time?

She really didn't talk about herself so much. She asked a lot of questions about his business; made herself basically indispensable; got him hot, bothered and distracted...but what was her deal? For a minute, he was a little annoyed at himself for not asking.

Then he narrowed his eyes until the city-lit sky blurred and he let the most unsettling thought settle right down on him.

What if Anna wanted...*information?*

The leak at Garrison had started about three or four months ago, right when she'd moved into the desk outside his office. She'd been promoted from HR, where, according to his department manager, she'd been an exemplary, if low-profile, employee.

But, still.

Ice hardened in the very veins that had been molten just minutes earlier.

Was Anna the spy?

Evidence, however circumstantial, started flashing like frozen images of proof in his head. She knew about every deal that had fallen through in the last two months. Of course she did; she had total access to his office. She'd even showered in there! How often had she been in there alone?

The only people who knew he was coming to London were the charter-jet people, maybe someone in his travel department…and Anna. And, in the elevator, she'd acted as if she'd never even heard of Jordan Jefferies, which seemed impossible in their business.

The impact of the revelation catapulted him to his feet, and he bounded back into the salon as the facts popped into his head and fell into place.

She knew the names of competitors. She constantly steered the conversation toward work. She always seemed so interested in the business, and even a little bit nervous around him.

Even on the plane yesterday, she'd dragged him back to open files, forcing him to go over every minor element of every major deal, and then, what had she done when they'd gotten to London? E-mailed it all. She'd said she was sending his e-mail for him, but was someone getting copied on that correspondence? Someone named *Jefferies?*

Oh, man. He almost cracked the crystal in his hand as he reviewed the events of the last hour. As soon as he'd talked about the spy, the minute he'd focused in on the mole in his operation, what had she done?

Classic, by-the-book, take-no-prisoners sexual distraction. Right up to the hotel room, she'd had him panting, pawing and as far away from thoughts of spies as he could be.

What did she take him for? He slammed the snifter so hard on the bar that brandy sloshed over the side and, in one move, he scooped up the master card key he'd left there.

What do you think I'm doing, Mr. Garrison?

He could still hear her seductive voice, feel the pressure of her kiss, the soft breath of a...traitor.

Jamming the card key into the lock on her bedroom door, his heart kicked against his ribs. And he froze. What if he was wrong?

Without making a noise, he turned the knob and opened the door. In the shadows, he saw her shape in the bed, the sheet almost covering her, but for one achingly long, sexy leg draped over it. He heard her sigh and shudder.

Already asleep...or faking it?

"Anna." His voice was sharp, demanding.

She jerked up, pulling the sheet over whatever she wore. "What do you want?"

He heard the tremor in her voice. Was that because she knew he'd figured out her game?

"Please, Parker, I'm sorry if I took things too far."

Disgust roiled through him. Did she really think he'd come in here and force her into having sex?

The sheet fell from her trembling hands, the moonlight revealing that she wore something tiny and strappy, like a tank T-shirt. Something easily lifted and removed.

Against everything he called *control,* his body responded. He was, after all, a man.

But not a stupid man. There was nothing to be gained by accusing her like this. He may have just leaped to one wild conclusion.

Swallowing hard, he gripped the doorknob. "I just wanted to make sure you're okay."

In the dim light, he could see that she very much doubted that was the truth. "I'm fine." She brushed a hair off her face. "Are you?"

The fact that she asked hit him somewhere deep, somewhere he'd rather not be hit by a woman he no longer trusted.

"Yeah. Good night." He closed the door and stared at it for a long minute.

He was probably right, and she was the spy. And if she was, then two could play this game. Now that he knew who his spy was, it was just a matter of feeding her misinformation. And if she really wanted to do her job for the Jefferies brothers well, she would probably have to get close to the CEO of Garrison, Inc.

Very close.

Parker Garrison may have been played for a fool by her this evening. But it wouldn't happen again. Next time, he'd get everything he wanted. *Every*thing.

And he wanted Anna. If he could crush Jordan and Emilio Jefferies in the process, all the better. But he could never let her know that he'd figured her out. In fact, the first thing he needed to do was let her wonder where she stood.

Anna Cross would find out the hard way not to play chess with a master.

Somehow, Anna made it through to Monday morning, but the magic of Saturday night seemed as far away as London when she tucked her handbag into her desk drawer and turned on the computer for the day.

"I didn't expect to see you here today." The receptionist appeared from the tiny galley kitchen that the Garrison executives shared, an empty coffeepot in hand.

"Of course I'm here," Anna said.

"Thought you might make a week of it across the pond." Sheila added a British accent to the last three words, and tempered the tease with a wink. "There were a few early calls this morning. The editor from *Luxury Travel* magazine called about the layout he's doing."

"Okay," Anna said, jotting a note. "Anything else?"

"The secretary at the charter-jet company called this morning to make sure Mr. Garrison *and* Ms. Cross had a pleasurable trip." Her voice was rich with implication and accusation. "So. Did you?"

"You can let them know that it was fine, thank you."

"You're holding out on me." Sheila laughed lightly. "Come on, spill the beans. Is he as demanding in bed as he is in the office?"

Anna managed a very disgusted glare, even though the memory of the moment he'd walked into her bedroom was still vivid. He could have demanded, and she might not have fought him. But he hadn't. And she'd barely slept once he'd backed out of the door, leaving her absolutely aching for more.

"Sorry to disappoint, Sheila. It was all business." Unfortunately. Fortunately. Oh, God, she was so confused.

"Oh, so it's like that, huh?" She beckoned Anna with the coffeepot and a very sympathetic smile. "Come here while I brew the mud. You look like you could use a friend."

Was it that obvious? Parker's distant coolness on the flight home had been a double-edged sword. It cut her because he was so icy, but it relieved her to know she could go back to work and a few steamy kisses had caused no real harm.

Obviously, he'd had a chance to think over the recriminations of an office affair and had decided she was too good an assistant to lose.

Or maybe he didn't want her.

The thought made her stomach squeeze with a sense of disappointment she had no right to feel. But he'd left her so confused. He'd hardly said six words to her on the flight, and three were *See you tomorrow.*

"Ever get involved with your boss before, Anna?" Sheila's question yanked her back to the present.

"No," she answered honestly. The boss's biggest rival, yes. And hadn't that turned out great? "It would be beyond dumb," she added.

Sheila rolled her eyes. "Tell me about it. I used to be a Playmate, did you know that?"

The entire company knew Sheila had worked as a bunny at the now-defunct Miami Beach Playboy Club. "I've heard that."

"Got all tight with one of the managers in the operation."

Anna wasn't entirely sure she wanted this much information, but couldn't help asking, "What happened?"

"What always happens," Sheila said with a world-weary exhale. "He got laid and I got canned."

"Oh."

Sheila nodded knowingly. "But, hey, it was fun while it lasted. That guy could…" She shook her head while she measured the coffee. "Let's just say he taught me some tricks that every girl should know."

"Would answering the phone be one of them?" Parker's voice was thick with sarcasm, eliciting a tiny gasp of surprise from Anna and a snort from Sheila. "Because my line just bounced from the main switchboard to voice mail after ringing about fifteen times."

Anna blinked at his tone. "Sorry, Mr. Garrison." She looked him directly in the eye as she passed through the narrow doorway and managed not to brush one fiber of his thousand-dollar suit. "I'll get your phone." She added some steel in her voice as she hustled toward her desk just as the next line rang.

"Mr. Garrison's office." His name rolled off her tongue,

flipping her stomach as the sight of him had done. This was why people shouldn't get involved at work. Forget what happened to her in the past. She couldn't even say his name without causing a mental meltdown.

"Hello." The voice on the phone was low, rich, female and unfamiliar. "I want Parker Garrison."

Get in line, Anna thought wryly. "May I tell him who is calling?"

"This is Cassie Sinclair Garrison, returning his call."

Anna corralled her scattered thoughts. Cassie Sinclair...*Garrison?* She was using the name now? That would put Parker in a fine...fin*er* mood. She turned just in time to see him heading into his office.

"Mr.—" She blew out a half breath. What did she call him now? Every time she said *Mr. Garrison,* they'd both think of his "warning" kisses. At least, she would.

"Who is it, Anna?" he asked, pausing at his door.

"Cassie Sinclair." No need to have him fume at her because his illegitimate half sibling was using her father's name. Let him find out on his own.

The color drained slightly from his sculpted cheekbones. "I'll take that call." He disappeared into his office, and closed the door with a definitive click, making her feel as shut out as he had on the plane when he'd slept or read the entire flight.

Behind her, Anna got a whiff of Sheila's spicy perfume.

"Not that it's any of my concern," she said, hitching a lazy hip against the arm of the guest chair. "But my experience tells me if you don't clear the air, then whatever is ricocheting off you two is going to do both of you in. And you'll cave first, darlin'."

"Nothing is ricocheting," she insisted. Except her heart. Why was he treating her like this? Would it be different if she *had* slept with him? Was he mad at her for saying no, or at himself for being…a man?

And what a man he was.

"Just clear the air, sweetie," Sheila said, giving Anna's hand a friendly pat. "Tell him you're sorry you did or you didn't, but don't lose your job over it if you can help it. No man's worth a paycheck, trust me."

As if she didn't already know that. "Thanks for the advice."

Sheila winked. "Anytime. And anytime you want to share the gory details…" She pointed toward the closed office door. "I bet that stud knows a few tricks, too."

"I wouldn't know," Anna said, her professional demeanor as secure as the button that held her modest shirt closed tight at the collar.

Sadly, Anna had to admit Shelia knew what she was talking about. As soon as that door opened, she was going to heed the unsolicited advice. She would tell Parker that despite the kisses and the chemistry they felt, they had to remain employer/employee only. But nothing else.

And once she told him that, she could get back to concentrating on her job. Maybe.

"Thank you for calling me back, Ms. Sinclair."

"Actually, I use both my last names. It's Cassie Sinclair Garrison." She ladled extra emphasis on their shared name and Parker just closed his eyes in revulsion.

But he refused to take the bait. "We need to talk about the questionable provisions in my father's will," he said, keeping any hint of emotion out of his voice.

The connection from Nassau was clear enough for him to hear her soft cough. "I'm not aware of any questionable provisions. It was all perfectly clear to me."

She was not going to be easy to manipulate. Well, of course not. Like it or not, she had Garrison blood in her veins and they were a stubborn bunch.

He powered on. "I think you'll agree that there's absolutely no reason for you to be bothered with the responsibility of twenty percent shares of Garrison, Inc. I've been running the company—"

"Not a bother at all," she assured him.

"I make the majority decisions for this company," he said firmly.

"I understand that and I hope you'll continue to do so," she said. "To be honest, I have no desire to exercise my new control, but I'll keep it. I have a hotel to run."

Relief washed over him. "Then I'll have my attorney arrange for you to rescind the shares immediately."

"That won't be necessary," she said coolly, as Parker stood and squinted into the Miami sunshine. "I have no intention of rescinding anything. I just don't want to exercise those shares right now."

He didn't like the sound of that. He didn't like the sound of any of this. "Then why not turn them over to me?"

"Because I don't want to."

She wanted money. Of course. "I will have my attorney draw up an extremely fair offer, Miss...Sinclair."

"It's *Garrison* and I wouldn't trouble your attorney because I will not sell my shares for any price, fair or otherwise."

"Why not?" She had to know he'd offer her well above market value.

"Because they were a gift." She paused for a moment, then added, "From my father."

Parker swallowed the bitter, metallic taste of fury in his mouth. "From your illegitimate father," he ground out.

"Be that as it may, he was and will always be a father to me. You may not know this, Mr. Garrison, but your father spent a lot of time in Nassau and he took very good care of my mother and me."

Forget apathy. Forget leaving family emotions at the door. This woman was doing everything in her power to incense him. And it was working.

"Is that so?" he replied. "Frankly, no one in my family—including *my mother, the one and only Mrs. John Garrison*—was aware of that."

She was quiet long enough to know he hit a mark. "Mr. Garrison, I'm going to make this very easy on you," she finally said.

"How's that?"

"Let's not talk anymore. If you have anything, absolutely anything, to say to me, put it in writing. I don't want to discuss business with you. I don't want to rescind my shares. I don't want to sell my shares. I don't want to hear about your mother. I don't want to meet your brothers and sisters and have a cozy family reunion. Is that clear?"

Oh, she was a Garrison, all right. He didn't even have to see the cleft in her chin to know for sure. "Crystal clear."

"Good. And don't try some underhanded, sneaky way to get rid of me. My father told me you can be ruthless."

He could be ruthless, all right. And would be, if necessary. "I have no idea what you're talking about."

"I know how much this means to you," she snapped back. "I don't put anything past you."

She didn't know anything about him and what meant what to him. "Excuse me, but you're the one who appeared out of nowhere claiming to be a Garrison."

She choked, her own temper obviously torqued. "I haven't appeared out of nowhere. I've been right here, for twenty-seven years, the daughter of John Garrison and Ava Sinclair. There were no 'claims.'"

"You'll have to prove it." The words were out before he could stop himself, erupted by his boiling blood. "We want to run full DNA tests and until conclusive proof is on my desk, my father's will is being contested in court."

He heard her breath escape in frustration. "Fine. Sic your lawyers on me. I don't care. Let me run my property the way I always have. Garrison, Inc. will get the appropriate percentage of my profits. In the meantime, stay away from me and I'll stay away from you."

She clicked off before he could respond. Swearing softly, Parker threw his phone on the desk and strode toward the door, his command that Anna get Brandon Washington on the phone already forming in his mouth.

He whipped the door open and almost knocked her down.

What was she doing there? *Listening?*

He glared at her, and she backed up a step, but lifted up her chin defiantly. "I want to talk to you."

Of course she was listening. The Jefferieses would probably want a full report. He gave her a smile, which wasn't difficult because even behind those little glasses, she was pretty. Very pretty.

"About what?" he asked, keeping his tone friendly.

She took a deep breath and glanced at the clerk who was slowly unloading the morning mail in front of her desk.

"Morning, Mario," Parker said, greeting the man who'd worked for the company since the year his father had opened it.

"Mr. Garrison." He nodded slowly, obviously more interested in the conversation than delivering the mail.

"Please," Anna said to Parker, starting to close his door. "It's personal."

But he put his hand on the wood to keep it open. "How personal?"

She speared him with a look. "Very personal."

He dipped one inch closer and the color immediately rose to her cheeks. For a spy, she sure had a weak spot. Several of them, in fact. One behind her ear, one just at the rise of her breasts and the weakest of all, the soft inside flesh of her thigh.

His body stirred at the thought. Might be time to exploit those weaknesses. "Then why don't we discuss it over dinner, Anna?"

Her eyes widened. "Dinner?"

"Yep. I feel like celebrating."

"You do?"

He cocked his head toward the phone on his desk. "It appears all the problems have been solved," he said smoothly. "Cassie Sinclair is going to rescind her shares. So, let's celebrate."

It wasn't really a lie. He'd win this and Cassie would rescind her shares, or sell them to him. But it wouldn't hurt to see if a little misinformation got dripped into the Jefferies organization.

"Oh, that's wonderful." She brightened, sounding very sincere. How would it sound when she relayed that information to Jordan and Emilio Jefferies? "Would you like me to get Brandon Washington on the phone for you?"

Damn, she was good. Spy or not, she had a skill for anticipating everything he needed. How would that translate in bed? The thought tightened his gut.

"Yes, please. And call Brittany Beach Restaurant and tell my sister to get us the best table in the house tonight."

"All right. Then we'll talk tonight."

They would. And he would plant a few more decoy

targets and then he'd sit back and watch Anna, and Jordan and Emilio, try to hit them. "I'll look forward to it."

The only problem was, he would. All day.

Five

Parker left the office early, met off-site with Brandon and made it to Brittany Beach well in advance of his "date." At seven, the sprawling veranda that overlooked the white sands of Miami Beach was already jammed with the beautiful people ready to blow off summer steam and partake in the edgy atmosphere.

He strode across the whitewashed planks, his sunglasses hiding his observation of a young woman in a bikini top so small a strong wind would loosen it. His sister Brittany had taken a lukewarm restaurant that had little going for it but a primo location and turned it into a fairly sizzling place to dine and be seen. Although Adam's Estate was the late-night destination for the younger club-going set, Brittany Beach had potential.

However, the potential Parker saw was primarily in the fact that the restaurant was located on one of the last waterfront parcels in SoBe still zoned for condos.

Still, Brittany was squeezing what she could out of the restaurant business. Unless it was pouring, the elegant Haitian cotton sofas under cabana tents were populated with self-absorbed Euro models and the men who liked to buy them drinks and dinner. This evening was no different.

"Hey, Parker. Over here." He turned at the sound of Stephen's voice, to see his brother sitting comfortably on one of those sofas, with no model in sight. There would be, eventually.

"'Sup, Stephen." Parker ambled over, offered his knuckles in greeting and took the silent invitation to join him. "You having dinner here?"

"Just stopped by to see how Brittany's doing. Have you seen her?"

"No, but I just walked in. She'll be around."

A pretty blond cocktail waitress in a revealing halter top and low-slung sarong sidled up to their table and flashed a smile. "Hi, guys. What'll it be?"

"I'm having dinner," Parker said, "but not for a few minutes, so just a bottled water for me."

Stephen ordered a light beer and asked if Brittany was around.

"She's in the kitchen," the waitress said. "You're her brothers, right? I'll tell her you're here."

When the waitress left, Parker slipped off his shades to look at his brother.

"How was the water this weekend?" he asked, knowing that Stephen, although he was as much of a workaholic as Parker, spent every free minute on his elegant cruising yacht.

"Gorgeous. A great escape from the mess that has become Garrison."

Parker acknowledged that with a puff of disgust. "You got that right. I talked to our newest sister today."

Stephen yanked his own sunglasses off. "And?"

"And she's added *Garrison* to her last name."

"Oh, man. What did she say?"

"In a nutshell, she won't rescind her shares, won't sell them outright, doesn't want a family reunion and would like to be left alone to run her property." Parker crossed his ankles and peered at the blue-on-blue horizon. "Brandon's filed the legal papers. I'm contesting."

"I don't know if you need it legally, but you have my support."

Parker nodded. "Thanks, bro. God knows if I'll have the others'."

"Adam will back you. And Brooke. I think, anyway."

"What do you mean? What's up with Brooke?" Parker had a well-known soft spot for his sister. "Is she still upset about the will?"

"About the fact that Dad had another family, oh yeah. I tried to talk to her about it, but you know Brooke. She's private."

"I'll give her a call," Parker said.

"You know, I think she's seeing someone, too."

"Really? Did she mention that at the Sunday dinner I missed?"

"No, in fact, she denied it," Stephen said. "But I know I saw her at the Grand last Thursday."

"The day of the will reading?"

"That night, actually. I saw her across the lobby, and some guy had his arm around her. Then he disappeared around the corner with her."

"And you never saw him before?" Parker leaned forward, his brotherly protective streak ignited.

"I only saw him from the back and when I asked her

about it on Sunday, she said I must have confused her with someone else."

"Brittany?"

"Brittany was here that night."

Brooke wouldn't lie, so Stephen must have been mistaken. "I'll have to talk to her, but still, I think she'll support my decision to contest the will. Not sure about her evil twin, though."

Stephen laughed softly. "Brittany's always a wild card." He glanced around as though just mentioning their sister would conjure her up. "I guess it depends what Garrison, Inc. wants to persuade her to do with this restaurant."

Parker shrugged. "I know this is her baby, and I was just thinking she's done a fine job bringing this place into the twenty-first century."

"It's profitable."

"On paper, yes. But do you have any idea how many more millions we'd get if we used this slice of land for condos?"

Stephen conceded that with a nod, saying nothing as the waitress delivered their drinks.

"She'd be devastated if we go that route," Stephen finally said. "You'd have to evict her, technically."

"I know, and I won't unless we're forced to. As long as she's turning a real profit here—and I mean a significant profit—then we can wait. But Garrison, Inc. owns the land, even if she owns the restaurant. If we wait, all that'll happen is that the cost of building will rise, and we'll charge five million for a condo instead of four. But if her business starts to falter, which, knowing the cyclical nature of the restaurant trade, it inevitably will—"

Behind him, a small but firm hand landed on his shoulder.

"Nothing is inevitable." Brittany's voice was as cold as the water he sipped. "Except that yet another poor, unsuspecting fool is up at the hostess stand asking for you. Haven't I seen this one before, Parker?"

She'd heard everything. He knew it. He'd just effectively put his sister on notice. What would that do when it came time for her support in contesting the will? He planted a smile and stood to greet her.

"Of course you've seen her before," he said, reaching to give her a brotherly, if cursory, hug. "She's my administrative assistant."

Brittany ignored his outstretched hands by putting hers on her slender hips. "That's Anna?" She frowned deeper. "She looks different."

"So is this a date or a business meeting?" Stephen asked.

Parker pulled his sunglasses back on. "A little of both, my friends. A little of both."

They both opened their mouths to speak, but he slipped away with a half salute of goodbye before they could bombard him with questions he didn't want to answer.

Anna saw his silhouette before she could make out Parker's face as he walked toward her, backlit by the early evening sun reflecting off the water. He moved like an athlete, so strong and in control of every muscle. He held his head high, his broad shoulders erect, his expensive suit draping perfectly over the body it was cut and sewn to fit.

When, she wondered, would this man stop taking her breath away?

She'd taken the job as his assistant knowing full well that she found him attractive. That hadn't seemed like something that would be crippling. She thought it would add a nice, interesting dimension to her job—the handsome boss.

But she hadn't counted on him being so down-to-the-bone appealing. And she certainly hadn't thought he'd ask her to travel with him and then kiss her senseless.

Of course, to be fair, she had kissed him first.

And there had been nothing *senseless* about it. She'd distracted him. And it had worked. But now they were going back to a strictly business arrangement that would stifle her attraction, and protect her from his digging into secrets that had to remain buried.

As Parker approached, his gaze dropped, quickly but clearly, and his eyebrows twitched in a silent compliment.

"You changed," he said with a smile. "I like that dress."

She'd chosen something black, simple, ladylike. But the way he inspected her, she wondered if he could see right through it. "I had a little time, so I took a run when I got home."

"How long have you been running?" he asked.

From the past? Darn near five years. "I started in high school," she said. "Got hooked on the endorphin rush."

His lips tipped in a smile. "I know the feeling."

"But you get it from work," she replied.

"I get it from a lot of things," he said, his voice so low and rich with implication she actually curled her toes as a hostess approached them.

"Inside or out, Mr. Garrison?" she asked, her sky-blue eyes trained on him flirtatiously.

But he didn't seem to notice. Instead, he put a confident hand on Anna's back and spoke to her. "I suggest we eat indoors because it gets a little raucous on the patio. Unless you'd prefer outdoor air."

"Inside is fine," she said.

"It's more private," he added, stepping a little closer. "Since you wanted to talk."

Yes, she did. And she couldn't let that glint in his dark chocolate eyes or that sexy, musky scent distract her from what she'd come here to tell him.

In a few minutes, they were seated in an alcove more like a bed than a booth, with a sheer privacy drape and a low table that practically begged the occupants to lie down and eat.

"Yeah, this is private, all right," she said, tugging at the skirt that rode up her thighs as she situated herself.

"We can leave the drape open, if you prefer," he said, shaking off his jacket and loosening his tie. She tried to swallow, but her throat had turned bone-dry and her hands itched to undo that tie even farther.

"Need a drink, Anna?" he asked as if he noticed her problem.

"Just water, please. I'm not drinking tonight." She needed every last wit to deal with him.

He ordered them both bottled water, which was delivered with tall, free-form cobalt-blue glasses of ice with curls of lemon and lime. While they sipped, he made small talk, mentioning that he'd seen his brother outside, telling her how the restaurant had changed since his sister had taken over ownership.

"Are you close to Brittany?" she asked, suddenly curious. "She doesn't call you much."

"We have our moments," he told her with a wistful smile. "She's definitely the more opinionated of the twins."

He told her a story from their childhood, something that proved his point about the difference between the twins, and Anna tried to concentrate on the details, but every minute or so her mind would drift to study the full shape of his lips, the marked cleft in his chin so like the ones all his siblings had.

He continued the story and she caught a few snatches, but her gaze slipped to his hair, which was short but thick and a little longer in the front, so that when he lowered his head, a single lock would fall on his forehead.

And his hands. God, she adored those hands. Like the feet, they were all size and strength. She watched his fingers close over the base of the water glass and remembered how they'd felt on her thigh, branding her with heat and desire.

"Can't you just imagine a seven-year-old girl doing that?" he asked.

A little wave of panic dried her throat again. She had no idea what he'd said. "No," she replied, hoping it was the right answer.

His smile was slow and teasing. "No, you can't imagine, or no, you didn't hear a word I said?"

Did he have to be so damn charming? That wasn't making this any easier.

Before she could answer, he leaned on one hand, the one that was perilously close to her hip, and trained that hot, dark gaze on her. "So, what's on your mind, sweetheart?"

Sweetheart. The endearment almost ripped her in half. Pulling up all her inner strength, she opened her mouth to say, "We have to be friends," just as Brittany Garrison arrived at the table, carrying a plate of sushi appetizers.

"I hate to interrupt this obviously important business meeting, but my chef has outdone himself in your honor." She set the plate between them, but looked at her brother. "We wouldn't want to *falter* in the kitchen now, would we?"

Parker plucked a tuna roll and winked at her. "No, we wouldn't, Britt. Do you remember my administrative assistant, Anna Cross?"

Anna reached out to shake Brittany's hand. "Hello, Brittany."

Brittany gave her a thorough assessment. "Of course we've met," she said warmly. "But you only worked for him then. How long have you been dating?"

"We're not—"

"Go away, Britt," Parker said, shooing her with a tuna roll. "It's bad business to annoy the patrons."

She merely shot him a sideways glance. "I need to know what night you want to reserve this place for Mother's sixtieth surprise bash."

He popped the sushi and chewed, wiping his mouth with a linen napkin and nodding in approval. "Nice, fresh fish, Britt. Compliments to the kitchen."

"What night, Parker? I have a business to run so I need to know when I can and cannot accept reservations."

"Accept everything. We're not doing it here. Adam's having it at Estate."

Brittany's elegant, sculpted jaw dropped and she snapped her arms across her chest. "We decided—"

"Adam convinced me."

"Or you made another wholesale decision without discussing it with anyone else."

He shrugged. "It makes way more sense to have it there. The party is a critical PR move for the family." For a moment, he paused and glanced at Anna, as though he wasn't sure he wanted her to hear that. "So, we're having it there."

Brittany's eyes narrowed, Anna obviously forgotten in the midst of a Garrison family squabble. But Parker didn't even notice. Because his decisions were made and abided, Anna thought. And never second-guessed.

By anyone.

Just like, she thought with a sickening wave of clarity, Michael Montgomery. Reminding her of why she'd come to this restaurant with this man: to stop any personal relationship before it started.

"Have a tuna roll, Anna," he said, sliding the plate closer to her. "Let's take this up in private, Britt. This isn't fair to Anna. How 'bout the house special tonight. Would you handle the ordering for us, so we can talk?"

Brittany nodded. "Of course. Enjoy your dinner," she said coolly. "And your date."

Anna sat up a little straighter. "This isn't a date," she said, her words making Parker freeze in the act of reaching for sushi. "But I'm sure we'll enjoy your lovely restaurant."

The corners of Brittany's mouth curled up and she gave Parker a raised eyebrow. "You do that." Without another word, she left the table.

In a move so smooth and fast, Anna almost didn't see it, Parker flipped the drape and shrouded them in gauzy privacy.

"What do you mean this isn't a date?" he asked, his voice only half-playful.

For a moment, she thought he was going to punctuate that question with a kiss, as though that would prove it was most certainly a *date*.

"I guess it's time for us to talk," she said, squaring her shoulders even more. "And please don't interrupt me."

He just lifted a brow, silent.

"I've given this a lot of thought," she started. "Since…Saturday. Since London." Since we kissed. But she didn't need to say that. The thought was reverberating through the small, tight space they occupied. "I think what happened was…" Amazing. Provocative. Tempting. "Not a great idea."

Still, he said nothing, focusing on her so intently, she could feel it singe her skin.

"I like my job," she continued. "I actually love my job. And I'd like to keep it. So, I want to…forget what happened. I'd like to be friends, of course. But you are my boss and I work for you and anything else is out of the question."

She paused, long enough for him to respond. But still, he just looked at her, his gaze wicked and direct. Until it dropped to her mouth and threatened to take her breath away.

"Don't you agree?" she finally asked.

"No." He dipped his head, the word almost lost as he lowered his head, slowly, intently, and kissed her, leaning so far into her that she almost fell back on the bedlike seat. His tongue teased her lips apart as he wrapped both arms around her and pulled her into his chest, the hammering of his heart as shocking to her as the complete ownership his mouth had taken.

Finally, after her ears sang with pounding, pulsing blood, he released her.

"I don't agree," he said, a sneaky smile tipping his lips just before he kissed her again, gently this time, mouth closed, eyes open. "I do not agree at all."

"Don't make this hard for me," she whispered. "You know I like to kiss you. You know I'm attracted to you. But I want to keep my job."

He backed away, just an inch, the playfulness gone from his eyes as he studied her. "Why is that so important to you?"

"Because it's how I make a living."

"Is that the only reason?"

She frowned, confused. "Yes."

"You're not…" He leaned his head in question. "Involved with another man?"

She shook her head, regarding him warily. "I wouldn't have even kissed you in London if I were."

"So there's no other man in your life."

Parker was a possessive man. Was that the reason he was forcing this angle? "No," she assured him. "There hasn't been for a long time."

"And you have no other source of income?"

She blinked at him. "Of course not. I make my living working for you."

"All right, then, I understand what you're saying." He reached for another sushi and gave her a wistful smile. "But I don't have to like it."

She sighed with relief. "I appreciate your respecting my concerns. I know you're a man who gets and takes whatever he wants."

His eyes flashed at that. "If I were, I would have taken what I wanted Saturday night. I wanted…" He closed his eyes in correction. "I *want* you."

"I wanted you, too," she admitted softly, resisting the urge to put it in the present tense. "But I want my job more."

He took a bite of the sushi, still studying her intently. "It's not the only administrative job in Miami, you know," he finally said. "I could help you find another just as good if you really want…to remove that obstacle."

The comment tore her in half. On one hand, the compliment ran deep. He really did want her—enough to try to help her past the hurdle that kept them apart. But on the other hand, she didn't want to risk the search into her background, the hassle and worry of getting another job.

She'd landed this one with the help of a trustworthy friend, but what might get revealed if she hit the job market?

Still, it seemed like a magnanimous gesture on his part. "Would you do that just so we could sleep together?"

"Trust me, there'd be very little sleeping involved." His smile was sinful.

"No." She shook her head in determination. "I want to work for you. I want to stay where I am. I'm learning a lot."

"You're learning a lot," he repeated slowly, the disappointment clear in his expression. "Well, if you change your mind…"

"You'll be the first to know," she assured him. "In the meantime, let's stay focused on business."

His smile was tight and forced, as if he didn't like what he was hearing at all. Another compliment. "Yeah," he said drily. "So you can *learn* more."

He opened the drape with a slow swipe as the waiter approached with their dinner. When it was served, Anna felt the strain of silence.

"You know," she said conversationally, "I was so busy this afternoon I forgot to check your calendar before I left. What's on it tomorrow?"

As he took a sip of water and swallowed, she watched the wheels turning, probably visualizing his PDA screen.

"I have an early-morning meeting with some developers of that North Miami property I've had my eye on."

"Really?" She tried to picture his calendar for herself. "I don't remember arranging that."

"You didn't." He studied his food intently, that stray lock falling on his forehead, tempting her to touch it. "I set it up myself."

"Oh. So you won't be in until, when? Ten?"

He gave her a quick look through his thick lashes. "Yep. Enough time for you to shower in peace."

She laughed softly, grateful for his humor. He may like to be in charge, but Parker had another side to him. A side that was much more human and tender than a man like Michael Montgomery. A very attractive side.

He held a forkful of his roasted duck toward her. "Want to taste?"

It wasn't entirely professional, and it wasn't a move that "friends" made, but she couldn't resist. She ate off his fork and the intimacy of the act pulled at her most feminine core, twisting a pang of arousal exactly the way his demanding kiss had.

As he held her gaze and fed her, she couldn't help feeling that he knew exactly what he was doing to her insides. And he liked it. With Parker Garrison, knowledge was power.

Power she had no doubt he would use—and use creatively.

She knew she'd made the right decision, but she just couldn't escape the sensation that she just might have made her life even more complicated.

Six

"You didn't bring a picture?" Anna threw plenty of exasperation in her voice as she served a cup of coffee to the friend she hadn't seen for far too long. "I don't think I've seen a picture of your daughter since she was two."

Megan Simmons tossed some wavy red curls over her shoulder and tucked her feet under herself as she got comfortable in Anna's kitchen. "Well, Jade's three and a half now and trust me, she's gorgeous. She'll be the first to tell you."

Laughing, Anna bit back the next obvious question. *Who does she look like?* Megan had never revealed the father of her child and Anna respected that. Their friendship dated back to elementary school and one of the reasons it had lasted so long was that they knew when not to pass judgment on each other's actions.

And they knew when to help each other. As Megan had four years ago, when she'd left her consulting job in Miami and returned to Indiana exactly at the time Anna had been up to her earlobes in false accusations. It was Megan's connection with the director of human resources at Garrison, Inc. that had given Anna a much-needed escape, and because of Megan's strong recommendation, she'd been able to get the job without the usual deep background check.

There were times when friends just didn't ask, no matter how much they wanted to know. So, Anna brought the conversation back to the reason they had this unexpected Saturday morning to share some coffee and chat before Anna drove Megan to the airport. "So, how did the meeting go yesterday?"

Megan took a sip, her green eyes widening over the cup. "It was really an interview," she said as she swallowed. "My former boss offered me a partnership in his design firm."

"Wow, congratulations." Anna lifted her coffee cup in a mock toast. "That's wonderful, Megan."

"Thanks. It sure is tempting."

"I'd love it if you moved back here."

Megan's expression grew warm, but wary. "Yeah, it would be great to live near you again, but I don't know."

"You loved Miami when you lived here."

"I know. But Jade has only ever known life in Indianapolis. And she's starting preschool this fall."

"The best time to move," Anna said. "You can start her here. Garrison, Inc. donates to an excellent private preschool. I bet I could get Parker to pull some strings and get Jade in there."

Megan pulled back, a little smile tugging at her lips. "Do you know that since I got here about twenty minutes ago, you've mentioned Parker Garrison about six times?"

Busted. "Have I? I hadn't noticed."

"I did," Megan said drily. "So I guess you're enjoying your promotion from the humble HR department to the lofty executive suites."

"It's different up there," Anna admitted. "It's more exciting. And I'm so busy. It's my whole life."

"It's your *job*," Megan corrected gently, using a voice she probably used on Jade when the child wanted soda instead of milk. "And I didn't say you mentioned Garrison, Inc. I said you mentioned your boss."

"I guess I have. But he's…" How could she possibly explain what it was like to work for someone like Parker?

"He's a Garrison," Megan said, rolling the name on her tongue as if it tasted bad.

"Yes, he is," Anna agreed. "And he's also…" She willed herself not to turn all dreamy and stupid. "Very…"

"Arrogant."

"Well, sometimes. But he's…"

"Demanding."

Anna's eyes widened. "He likes things his own way, but he can be…"

"A snake."

Her jaw dropped. "No. I don't think he's a snake, Megan. He's confident and a leader, he's smart and he's—"

"Flat-out gorgeous. They all are." Megan took a deep drink then thunked the cup back on the table. "Don't get sucked into it, Anna."

"Sucked into what?"

Megan leaned on the table. "I've done enough work for the Garrisons to know what they're made of."

"You consulted, Megan, as the interior designer when they refurbished the Garrison, Inc. offices. You don't really know them. It's not the same as being in their face day after day."

"Oh, I was in their face plenty," she volleyed back, more blood deepening the delicate dusting of freckles across her nose. "Don't forget what happened to you, Anna. You are a living example of what can happen to a woman who is wooed by a man who isn't above using her," Megan said.

"He hasn't used me," she said, defensiveness making her voice tighten as she stood. "And I already gave him the 'we can only be friends' speech this past week at dinner and he's been nothing but business since then."

"It's gone that far? You had to give him that speech?"

"Not that far," Anna mused, turning off the oven and taking a minute to refresh their cups. "We've only kissed. In London. That's all, I swear."

Megan held her cup for a refill. "Why?"

"Why was that all or why did we kiss?"

"Oh, I know why you kissed," Megan said wryly. "You kissed because you were in a ridiculously romantic place and wildly attracted to each other and he whispered in your ear and you melted."

Anna laughed as she put the coffeepot back and sat. "Oh, you think you know everything."

"Not everything. But I know enough."

The need to share the truth was powerful and if anyone would understand, Megan would. "We kissed because he told me he suspects there's a spy in the company and I planted one on him to drag him away from that dangerous train of thought."

"A spy?" Megan's eyes popped. "No wonder you're freaked."

"Can you imagine if he found out that I was stupid enough to let my boyfriend infiltrate my boss's computer system and steal technology secrets at my last job? And then got blamed for it?"

"You'd be okay," Megan said. "I mean, you've been at Garrison for four years or so."

"But now there's the Internet. How long would it take before someone searched my name and found articles in the local Indianapolis papers accusing an administrative assistant of being a corporate spy?"

"You were innocent, Anna. Michael Montgomery finally admitted he did it."

"Yes, I know that and you know that, and even my former boss knows that because the confession happened in the privacy of a conference room in Indianapolis."

"Barry Lynch dropped all charges."

She nodded. "Yes, he did. The boss dropped the charges and the boyfriend fled town and no one bothered to call the papers and inform them except me, and the reporter wasn't interested. Called it an 'old story.' But my name is still media mud."

Megan sighed, obviously unable to deny that. "Barry Lynch is still running FiberTech outside of Indy. Why don't you call him and ask him to vouch for you?"

"I don't want to dredge up old history. He was embarrassed by the lax security in his company, anyway. That's why he didn't tell the newspapers the truth." Anna closed her eyes. "I want it all behind me."

"I know you do." Megan reached across the table and put her hand on Anna's. "And I want you to be careful with Parker Garrison."

Parker again. "Do you even know him, Megan?"

"I met all the Garrisons when I did the consulting job. Cheating runs in their genes."

"Cheating?" Then Anna recalled the latest Garrison scandal. "I guess you're right." She rose and donned an oven mitt to slide the pastry tray out, and as she did, told

Megan the whole story of Cassie Sinclair and her unlikely role at Garrison, Inc.

Megan listened, rapt, then asked, "So this woman over in Nassau is John Garrison's illegitimate daughter?"

"Looks that way. And now she owns twenty percent of Garrison, Inc."

Megan's eyebrow notched. "At least he took care of his child."

At the catch in her friend's voice, Anna turned from the oven, pastry tray extended, but Megan hid her expression behind the coffee cup.

"Would you like a cinnamon roll?" Anna asked.

Megan put her cup down with a little too much force. "But you see what I mean?" she asked, obviously not hearing Anna's question. "See what they're made of? Gorgeous, yes, every last one of them. But can they be trusted? And you, after all you've been through, you have to trust the man you love, Anna."

The tray slipped in Anna's mitted hand, but she caught it. Love. *Whoa.*

"This isn't love," she managed to say. "This is a pathetic crush on my part and lust on his."

Megan's chair scraped the tile as she stood. "You think? How's he treated you since you gave him the speech?"

"Well, he's had a lot of closed-door meetings and placed most of his own calls, so I thought he was trying to avoid me. But…" Her voice trailed off as she tried to think of how to explain what had been happening for the past five days. "But when we're together, well, to be honest, there's been a lot of electricity in the air."

"Oh, really?" Megan meandered over to the counter to help herself to a cinnamon roll. "Like lightning bolts that turn your lower half into liquid and your brain to mush?"

"Yeah." Anna half laughed.

"And every time your hands casually brush when you exchange papers, you sort of shiver and get all tingly?"

"Precisely."

Megan took a bite of gooey pastry, nodding like a knowledgeable expert as she chewed. "And," she added when she swallowed, pointing the roll at Anna, "when he laughs at something you said, the whole room sort of spins and your heart gets all fluttery and your arms get numb from the need to touch him?"

"Every time."

Megan slid her finger along the top of the cinnamon roll, covering it with icing. "You're in love," she pronounced.

"No, I'm not. I'm just in big, fat trouble."

Megan sucked the icing off her finger with a noisy smack and a knowing grin. "Same thing."

The last thing Parker wanted to do on Sunday was trudge up to Bal Harbor for the weekly Garrison dinner. Not that driving Collins Avenue with the top of his BMW M3 down and his floorboard-rumbling stereo at full blast was exactly *trudging,* but he still would rather have spent the evening working on the endless pile of paper that seemed to accumulate on his desk that week.

Because, God knows, he hadn't gotten anything of consequence accomplished at work since Monday. Unless playing games with Anna Cross was "work."

He'd planted three separate false trails regarding business development, and not one of them had resulted in sending the Jefferieses on a wild-goose chase.

He'd tried to draw Anna out from her cloak of professionalism, teasing her with the occasional joke and letting the inevitable contact blister into heat between them. But that hadn't accomplished anything except more than a few restless nights for him and a bad case of unrequited…arousal.

And that, he thought, popping out the classic-rock CD he'd been playing and searching his collection for something that suited his mood, was the problem.

She was getting to him.

Maybe it was her resistance to his obvious interest. Maybe it was the fact that he suspected her of spying and couldn't seem to catch her. Maybe it was the memory of those few kisses, that promise of so much more in London.

He shifted uncomfortably in his seat, the all-too-familiar southbound rush of blood reminding him that whatever the hell it was about Anna Cross, it had an undeniable effect on him.

No matter which way he cut it, rationalized it or ignored it, he still wanted her. A lot.

His fingers grazed the CD cases restlessly, skipping each one. If not rock or jazz or a decent piano concerto, what did he want to hear?

Broadway tunes.

"Oh, man." He tapped the steering wheel and yanked left into the stone gates of the Garrison estate. "That's bad, Garrison. That's rock-bottom bad."

He whipped into an open space behind Adam's smaller model BMW and checked his rearview, raking his hands through his wind-whipped hair in self-disgust. Since when did he have the slightest interest in Rodgers and Hammerstein?

Since that little vixen hummed show tunes while she was filing. Off-key, no less. But when she tapped her toes to some ditty that ran through her head and the tip of her tongue sneaked out between her sweet, soft lips, the next thing he knew he had a sudden need to—

"Don't worry, you're perfect." Brooke leaned over the passenger door of the convertible and offered her brother a friendly grin. "Making all the girls wild, as usual."

He reached over and gave her hand a squeeze. "I'm afraid it's the other way around lately."

That earned him a surprised lift of her shapely eyebrow. "Don't tell me someone's finally gotten under big, bad Parker's skin."

"Not a chance," he assured her, popping out of the car and coming around to give her a hug. "But who are *you* sneaking around with these days?"

All the color drained from Brooke's usually rosy cheeks. "What?" She half laughed and accepted his hug. "You must have me mixed up with my far more social twin."

He released the embrace, but held her shoulders tightly and searched her face, a pang of guilt twisting through him. He'd promised Stephen he'd call her this week and he hadn't even remembered. He'd been so caught up in…Anna.

"Are you okay?" he asked, unwilling to let go of her shoulders. "Stephen told me you've been pretty miserable since the whole Cassie Sinclair thing came out."

Her eyes filled, but she blinked back the tears. "I'm having a hard time, Parker," she replied. "What Dad did was, well, unforgivable. And to let us know like that. During the reading of his will." She inched out of his grip with a shudder of anger.

He slid his arm around her as they crossed the brick driveway and approached the massive glass-and-mahogany entrance to the Spanish-style villa.

"I know how you feel," Parker commiserated. "Mad and hurt and disillusioned. And, hell, we're still in mourning.

I can't believe I'm going to walk into this house and he isn't going to be on the back veranda, drinking in the ocean view, ready to dissect every nuance of the past workweek and plan the attack for the next one."

She raised her delicate jaw so the sunlight caught the dip of the Garrison cleft in her chin. "That's your job now, Parker."

"Don't I know it," he said, the weight of the "patriarch" role weighing heavy on his shoulders. "Those are big shoes to fill."

"No problem," she assured him with a gentle elbow to the ribs. "You've got big feet."

Before they even reached the last of the wide stucco stairs that led to the entrance, the doors opened and Lisette Wilson, the real keeper of the Garrison house, appeared in her standard navy-and-white uniform, looking a bit older than her fifty-five years.

The loss of John Garrison had hit their longtime house-keeper hard, but Parker knew that something more than that was working on Lisette.

"Hello, Lisette," he greeted her with a gentle hand to her shoulder, while she gave a nod to him and a peck on Brooke's cheek. "How are you?" Parker asked.

She answered that with pursed lips feathered with a dozen tiny creases. "I'm fine, Mr. Parker, but I can't say the same for your mother. The bottle has been open since eleven this morning."

He felt his sister sink into him. "Oh," Brooke said. "Thanks for the warning, Lisette."

Behind the housekeeper, Adam strode into the oversize entryway, a frown on his angular face. "I'm leaving," he said gruffly. "Sorry, but I'd rather be anywhere but here listening to her rant about Ava Sinclair."

"Ava who?" Brooke asked. "Is that Cassie's mother?"

"Yes," Parker said. "Brandon Washington has been doing some digging. The woman, Dad's, uh, friend, passed away about a month before he did."

"And I'm supposed to feel bad about that?" Bonita ambled in and leaned shakily on a wide stone column that marked the entrance to a sprawling living room, a glass of something potent in her hand. She shook a strand of hair off her face, revealing some makeup streaked under her eyes. "Maybe your father died of a broken heart when his mistress croaked."

Parker's heart sank. Mother was loud, rough and blasted.

Lisette immediately stepped to her side. "Why don't I take you upstairs to freshen up while the children gather, Mrs. Garrison," she said, as gently as if she were talking to a petulant toddler. "Mr. Stephen should be here soon, and maybe Miss Brittany. I daresay we'll have a full house tonight, and I made braised beef."

"I don't like braised beef," his mother whined, but she allowed herself to be led up a winding staircase, mumbling under her breath as she clutched the wrought iron railing.

Adam blew out a disgusted breath and continued toward the front door. "I'm outta here."

"Wait," Brooke said, going after him. "Come on, Adam. We need to be a family."

"You need to be a family," he shot back. "I need to be somewhere else." He opened the door to leave just as Stephen walked up the stairs. Wordlessly, Adam pushed past his brother with Brooke on his tail.

"Adam, please," she called. "She'll sober up."

"Just enough to insult you, Brooke."

"No, wait, Adam."

Stephen stepped aside to let his siblings barrel by, a bemused smile aimed at Parker. "Another Sunday in paradise, I see."

Parker shook his head. "For this, I gave up work."

Stephen laughed lightly and gave his brother a friendly pat on the shoulder. "Spoken like a true Garrison, bro. But I bet the old man isn't up in heaven saying, 'I should have spent more days at the office.'"

"What do you mean? You're as much of a workaholic as I am," Parker said as the two of them headed toward the back of the house, drawn by the scents of Lisette's cooking and the possibility of a relaxing, private moment together.

Out of habit, they went straight through the bank of French doors to the veranda. A cool breeze blew the dozens of queen palms that lined the limestone patio, exotic scents of tropical flowers wafting from the planters that surrounded an Olympic-size pool that no one actually used.

Stephen ambled to the marble-topped wet bar and poured two fingers of Dad's single malt into cut-crystal tumblers.

"In honor of the old man," he said, giving one glass to Parker and holding the other in a mock toast.

"We're as bad as mom," Parker said drily.

"Nah. This is my first and it's five o'clock."

Parker acknowledged that with a nod. "Yeah, yeah." But he barely sipped the hot, amber liquid, clunking the glass down on the bar. "It's been a helluva week."

Stephen pulled out a leather bar stool and settled next to his brother. "Tell me about it. The bastards are up to no good again."

"Jefferies? What happened?"

"Remember that photo spread in *Luxury Traveler* I negotiated for the hotel?" Stephen said. "Fourteen pages of priceless coverage in one of the top travel magazines in the world?

I worked with the editorial director, schmoozed him, wined him, dined him, let him stay in the penthouse with a young woman who was definitely not his wife. Remember?"

"Of course," Parker said. "That editorial coverage will be equivalent to a hundred thousand worth of ad dollars for the Grand."

Stephen snorted. "Not anymore. He's changed his mind and is waiting for Hotel Victoria to open. He's using *that* as the background for the photo shoot and story about the latest hip and hot hotels in South Beach."

"What?" Parker slammed his hand on the counter. "How did the Jefferieses swing that? No one even knew that story was in the works."

No one, he thought as the whiskey turned bitter in his mouth, but the woman who sat outside his office. Maybe some others, but he distinctly remembered Anna knew about the deal because the editorial director of *Luxury Travel* had called him on more than one occasion.

"I'm royally ticked," Stephen said. "But since it's not paid advertising, my hands are tied. He said it was strictly an 'editorial' decision."

Parker swore softly.

"We got a hole in the dam," Stephen said. "And we can't ignore it any longer."

Parker took a deep drink of the scotch. "I think I know who it is."

"You do? Who?"

He hesitated, but only for a moment. This was Stephen, and they had no secrets. "Anna."

"Anna Cross? Your secretary?" Stephen stabbed his fingers through his hair in disbelief. "Is that why you're dating her?"

"It didn't start out that way, but then she said and did a

few things that made me suspicious. Anyway, I'm not dating her. She wants to keep it all business."

"Sure, so she doesn't get fired and can keep her hands in your files." Stephen sounded disgusted. "What are you doing about it?"

"I've tried a misinformation campaign, but that isn't working. They didn't bite on anything this week."

"Then you'll have to use a James Bond technique," Stephen said, a half smile threatening. "Screw the truth out of her."

A tremor of heat warred with distaste. Not screwing, not with Anna.

"She's keeping me at arm's length," Parker said.

Stephen looked unconvinced. "Come on, ace. You can do this. You're a master."

"I really like her." The admission sounded a little lame, but felt amazingly good. He did like her. Wasn't that at the bottom of all his angst? It certainly explained the sudden desire to listen to the overture from *Camelot*.

"She's using you."

Was that even possible? She was so guileless. "I don't know that for a fact."

"Then find out." Stephen stood to make his point. "Forget misinformation or seduction. Set her up and catch her in the act. Then you can fire her and we can stop this infernal leaking of proprietary information."

Parker lifted his glass and swirled the remaining whiskey. "Seems kind of underhanded, don't you think?"

"And spying on us and feeding information to Jordan and Emilio Jefferies is aboveboard?" Stephen tapped him on his shoulder. "What do you think your father would do?"

John Garrison would have set her up and taken her

down in a heartbeat. Business before personal feelings. Business before *anything*.

"Hey, if she's innocent," Stephen added, "then you find that out, too. Then you can seduce her for real."

"Seduce whom?" Brittany strolled onto the veranda and sidled up to her two brothers. "Who's your next victim?"

"No one," Parker said dismissively.

His brother was right; they had to know the truth. The thing was, if he was wrong, and Anna realized he suspected her, he'd never have a chance with her. Ever.

But if he was right, then he'd be doing the very thing the patriarch of the family should be doing: protecting the Garrison brand.

When it came down to that, he really had no choice.

Seven

By five o'clock on Monday, Anna thought she'd jump out of her skin. Or jump onto her boss's. She'd spent every moment at work next to Parker, at times so close you couldn't slide a hair between them. He seemed to need—or want—her for everything. He had her in his office reorganizing files, requiring her to stay in the room during his telephone conversations so she could take down pertinent information.

He brought in lunch and while they ate, he discussed the possibility of launching an ad campaign for the brand, an idea she'd certainly heard him reject in the past.

Forget the ad campaign. Forget the sudden outpouring of business issues. When he reached over and took her pickle off her paper plate, grinned and asked seductively, "You don't mind sharing, do you?" Anna almost melted into his plush leather sofa. Which she had no right sharing with him, but that was where he'd set up lunch…like some kind of impromptu picnic.

Every overheated cell in her body ached from the torture of being so close without being able to touch, her senses bombarded with the pleasure of seeing him lean over a piece of paper to sign his name, that lock of hair nearly kissing his brow exactly the way she wanted to. Slack-jawed and weak-limbed and awestruck, she watched him shed his jacket at two, loosen his tie at four and unbutton his cuffs to reveal his powerful, broad wrists at five-thirty.

One more minute and she'd start on his belt buckle.

How long could this go on?

"Anna," he chided when his PDA dinged softly. "We forgot the business council meeting tonight."

"We did? I did?" She shuffled through the papers for his calendar. "I don't have a business council meeting on your schedule."

He started lowering the cuffs and buttoning them, sending relief and disappointment colliding through her.

"This meeting was added at the last minute by the board to discuss the next election," he told her.

"That must be why I didn't know about it," she said. That or the fact that she'd gone way past *distracted* and had slid right into *useless* ever since they'd gotten back from London.

Maybe she was trying to sabotage her job; if she didn't work for him, then she could act on all the chemistry she was absolutely certain she wasn't imagining.

If she didn't work for him, she could meet him here late at night and… Her gaze drifted to the leather sofa where they'd eaten lunch, her mind already imagining the stamp of his body on hers; the heat of his hands under her blouse; the wet, warm feel of his lips suckling her breasts—

"But it has to be done by tomorrow morning, so I'm afraid you'll have to finish it tonight."

What in God's name was he talking about? "Which will entail…?" She scanned his desk for a clue to what he'd just told her to do.

"The usual, complete the spreadsheets. It won't take you long. I'm sorry you have to work late. You didn't have plans did you?"

Not unless jogging off nine hours of sexual frustration and then spending the rest of the night fantasizing herself right back into that blissful state constituted *plans*. "No, not tonight."

"Good. To make it easier on you, I've left the data on my computer, so you can just input the spreadsheets right here." He indicated his desk. "You don't mind that, do you?"

Yes, she minded. She had to sit in his chair, his spicy aftershave lingering in the air, his computer under her fingertips. But what she really minded was that she had no idea what he was talking about.

"Um, Parker, which spreadsheet again?"

He laughed softly. "You seem a little distracted today, Anna. You okay?"

"I…I just…" She smoothed her hair and squared her shoulders. "Missing the business council on your calendar kind of threw me."

He waved it off and dragged the charcoal suit coat back on. "I'm referring to the monthly property report for the executive committee. All of the profits from Garrison companies are rolled into that report. My brothers and sisters will be in here tomorrow morning for the exec committee meeting and we'll go over it first thing."

"Oh, of course." Still she frowned, not remembering a document they'd done like that in the past. Didn't all the

Garrisons bring their numbers to the meeting individually, and announce them that morning? Why were they doing it this way?

He slipped some files—she was so distracted, she didn't even know *what*—into his soft-sided leather briefcase and gave her an unreadable look, almost as if he was a little disappointed. He probably was—she hadn't really done her usual bang-up job this week.

Plus, she was getting far less adept at hiding her attraction. Maybe he knew she said one thing to him about their physical relationship, but dreamed of another. Maybe he could tell she was really regretting her decision to keep their relationship strictly professional. Because she was. Deeply. Daily.

"I'll see you tomorrow, then, Anna." What was that expression on his face? Expectation? Hope? Uncertainty? Something was on his mind, but he wasn't saying. Was he hoping she'd change her mind, or had he moved on?

No. She wasn't imagining the sizzle between them.

"I'll be in at eight," she promised him. "And the meeting starts at nine."

He came around his desk and paused in front of her. Inches away, she could feel the heat of him, the sense that he was trying to tell her something nearly buckling her knees.

"Is there anything else, Parker?" Did he hear that note of need in her voice?

"No. There's nothing else." He lifted his hand and brushed a single stray hair from her face, the featherlight touch sparking her skin. Had he noticed she'd been wearing her hair down? "I just… I'm sorry."

"Sorry?" She pulled back. "For what?"

"Sorry you have to work late."

She let out a quick breath, almost a laugh. "I always

work late," she assured him. "And going to a business council meeting isn't exactly a fun time for all."

He smiled, cocking his head exactly the way he would if he were going to kiss her. Her heart walloped so hard, he had to have heard it. Had to have noticed her lips parting, her eyes half closing. He dipped a centimeter.

He was going to kiss her. Her fingers tightened on the papers she held; her gaze dropped to his mouth; her gut clenched in anticipation.

He was going to kiss her, and she was going to kiss him right back.

"Good night," he said gruffly, jerking himself away and marching across the office to the door.

Anna stood stone still for a full minute after the door slammed; the only thing moving was her poor, overworked heart as it tried to redirect blood back into her brain.

Finally, she sank into a chair and took a breath.

She had all night to do his spreadsheets. She needed that run in the worst way. The way she felt right now, she could tear down Biscayne Boulevard, cross the MacArthur Causeway and throw herself into the Atlantic Ocean and it wouldn't erase the fire and need in her body.

But she would try.

"I gave her plenty of rope," Parker said, taking a sip of the draft beer Stephen had just handed him. Instead of hops and wheat, he tasted misery. And regret.

"You gave her all fake numbers, right?" Stephen leaned back on Brittany Beach's comfortable couches as if he didn't have a care in the world.

He didn't, Parker thought drily. Stephen hadn't just arranged an elaborate setup that could ruin a woman he respected. A woman he liked.

A woman he wanted so bad he could howl at the rising moon.

"Yeah," Parker said. "Every single line item a lie." He checked his watch, imagining his dutiful secretary entering made-up profits into a spreadsheet. Would she e-mail that file directly to Jordan Jefferies?

"And you're sure she'll do the work on your PC, not hers?"

Parker nodded. "I set it up that way."

"And you're sure you installed the software?" Stephen prodded. "The one that tracks every keystroke?"

"Yes," Parker answered impatiently.

"Cool stuff, isn't it?"

"Very. I just wish I wasn't using it to bring down Anna."

"To bring down a *spy,*" Stephen reminded him. "I have that on my PC, too. It's just smart protection. Did you know it was invented by a private investigator?"

A P.I. That didn't make Parker feel any better about spying on the woman whose only sin might just be having perfect legs. And a killer smile. And beautiful hair. And that sweet laugh. And a sharp intellect. And—

"You're having second thoughts."

Parker sipped the beer, which still tasted flat and bad. "I'm way past second, bro."

"Hey, if she's the spy, this will be the smartest business move you ever made. You're a hero for trapping her."

He didn't feel like a hero. He felt like a heel. Keeping her close all day long, feeding her BS just to see if she'd spread his lies to the competition. And all the while, every time she moved or breathed or looked at him with all that unmistakable longing in her eyes, his whole being constricted with the fight not to take her in his arms and annihilate her with his mouth.

"What if someone else gets to my computer and it's not

even Anna?" he said as the bizarre thought took hold. "What if she gets blamed for something she didn't do?"

"What are the chances of that?" Stephen asked.

"Slim. None."

"Relax. Here comes Brittany." Stephen gave his sister an inviting wave. "Let's torture her."

But Parker's heart wasn't into teasing his sister, so he let Stephen and Brittany talk while he stared at the horizon.

A beautiful redheaded model glided by and gave him an interested smile, but he just looked past her, his mind seeing a different woman altogether. A little while later, Brittany introduced him to her newest waitress, Tiffany, and he barely noticed her generous cleavage, so she turned her charms on Stephen. Even the arrival of two Miami Heat cheerleaders didn't snag his attention.

Brittany brought him another beer. "Your first one's flat and warm by now." She picked up the barely touched pilsner glass. "If I didn't know you as an arrogant master of the universe, I'd say you were lovesick tonight."

Parker pulled his focus from the darkening Atlantic Ocean to his sister. "I'm not lovesick, Britt."

She laughed. "No argument on arrogant, I see." When he didn't respond, she added, "Then what's your problem?"

He swallowed the smart-ass retort he'd usually give his sister and just shook his head. "Business, of course."

"Of course," she said, perching on the rattan armrest of the sofa. "It's never anything else with you, is it?"

"What's that supposed to mean?" he asked.

She shrugged. "Just wondering if there's a heart in that big old chest of yours, or just a calculator."

Was that how he seemed? To her? To everyone? To Anna? The thought made his chest ache. Not the way a calculator would at all.

A customer called Brittany and she stood, giving Parker a rare squeeze on the shoulder. "Too bad you're such a machine, Parker. If you'd loosen up, I might actually like you."

He looked up, ready to remind his sister that she had the right to be flighty; she was the youngest. He, on the other hand, had the weight of the family name on his first-born shoulders. But Brittany had taken off, and Stephen was flirting with the new girl.

He'd had enough.

"Where are you going?" Stephen asked when Parker stood and set the new beer on the table with a thud.

"I'm leaving," he said vaguely.

Stephen frowned at him. "You changed your mind?"

Parker opened his mouth to argue, but just held up a hand. "I'm going to handle this my way." He hustled away before his brother could argue.

If she was the spy, he'd catch her in the act. Forget tracking her keystrokes and placing blame, he'd walk in and find her there, make her freeze before she had time to close whatever info she was stealing and then they could have it out.

He'd fire her and she'd be gone, no chance for an excuse.

This catching-her-with-software was just not his style.

Propelled by the need to take action, and maybe by the need to see her again, regardless of what he found her doing, Parker was in his car in no time. He zipped back over the causeway and whipped down Brickell toward his office. He parked underground in the high-rise and made it to the elevator in a few steps, his blood already spiked.

Would he tell her he'd set her up? Would she be gone already? The elevator seemed to drag up each of the twenty-two floors as his gut tightened in anticipation.

The soft ding of the elevator echoed in the empty hall. To his left, the wide glass doors of Garrison, Inc. were closed and locked, the reception area bathed in shadows formed by up lighting under the brass Garrison logo on one wall.

He had a key, of course, and turned it quietly, then locked the door behind him. He stood for a moment near Sheila's desk, listening. He heard nothing.

Could Anna be gone? Something like disappointment shifted in his stomach and he walked soundlessly down the hall to his office.

Anna's desk was empty, her computer off. But the file with the spreadsheet information was right on top. Curious, he opened it. It was untouched. She hadn't done it yet? In two hours? Had she spent the entire time raiding his computer?

His door was closed tightly and he paused, wondering if he should just use his key or jiggle the handle. The latter could alert her and she could quickly clear the screen.

But her moves would be tracked with the software.

He jiggled, but it was locked. Quickly, he slid his key in and with a dramatic thrust, pushed the door open.

The room was empty. A Garrison, Inc. logo danced around as a screen saver on his computer. That meant the computer had been untouched for at least half an hour.

He stepped toward his desk, and then he heard it.

High-pitched, heartfelt and as flat as a sick puppy. Singing.

She could have danced all night.

Audrey Hepburn might roll over in her grave at Anna's rendition of a signature song, but Parker Garrison simply froze and imagined the woman he wanted…wet, naked and belting out a ballad in the shower.

If she was a spy, he'd fire her. If she wasn't, he'd…

Join her.

In two steps, he was at his keyboard, typing the password to access the results of some investigator's programming.

She hit a high note. It hurt.

He tapped a few more keys and there were the results. He blinked and leaned closer to make sure he was reading right. And he was. Anna Cross hadn't so much as touched his keyboard, even though she'd had two hours to raid about four dozen "proprietary" files on his hard drive.

Anna Cross wasn't the spy.

A slow, satisfied grin pulled at his mouth. He was so happy that he could kiss her.

He walked to the bathroom door, put his hand on the knob and decided he would do precisely that. And anything else she'd let him do.

Anna held her arms out until her fingertips touched either side of the slick marble walls. The dual shower heads pulsed rivers of warm water down her back and over her chest, giving her the sensation of being suspended in between two waterfalls. She dropped her head back, let her hair slide down her back and nailed the final note with a flourish even she had never obtained before.

The slow, rhythmic snap of one person's applause from the other side of the frosted-glass door hit her as hard as the water.

With a gasp, she twisted the knob that operated both heads.

"Please don't stop on my account."

Oh, God in heaven. *Parker.*

Adrenaline left her whole body quivering. He couldn't see her through the steamy glass, but she still covered her bare breasts automatically.

Taking a deep breath, she dug for a perfectly normal voice. "You said I could use the shower whenever I wanted."

"I did and I meant it. I see you went running."

She remembered her shorts and tank top dropped on the floor outside the shower. "Uh-huh," she managed to say.

Suddenly, a fluffy towel curled over the top of the shower door. "Here you go."

Anna glanced down at her body, her skin rosy from the heat, water still sluicing down her breasts and stomach, into the triangle of curls between her legs.

She shivered, despite the steam.

He was there. Parker. On the other side of that glass. And all she had to do was…open the door. Invite him in. Take what she wanted so much her whole being ached.

"Are you all right in there?"

She didn't answer him, unsure of what she might say, what shocking invitation she might issue if she opened her mouth.

"Anna? Are you okay?"

She reached toward the glass and placed one fingertip on the steam. That was all that separated her bare and willing body from him. One thin sheet of fogged-up glass.

"Why did you come back?" she finally asked.

Behind her, a drop of water hit the marble floor and another dribbled down the drain. Her finger trailed a thin line in the glass, clearing a quarter-inch view.

"I wanted to…check on you." His voice was low and seductive. And so close. He had to be just inches from the glass door.

"I'm fine." She made a second line in the fog. "See?"

His five fingertips touched the glass, leaving ovals where his skin pressed against it. "Yes, you are. Very fine."

She lifted her left hand, and matched his handprint, fingertip for fingertip. "And so are you." He might not have heard her, since she breathed the words.

"Anna." His fingers moved an inch, and she followed them.

"Yes?"

This was the part where he made a light joke about her voice or teased her about his shower. This was the part where he backed away and gave her privacy to change alone. This was the part where he reminded her that she had work to do and he was the boss and she was the—

"I want you to open the door."

Heat and desire rolled through her like the steam clouds in the shower. Her arm trembled, her chest tightened and everything in her that was female curled into a fist of longing low in her belly.

She pressed the door just hard enough to release the latch, but not reveal herself. The barrier was still there, but falling fast.

Through the opaque glass, she saw a dark jacket slide to the ground. The tie, the buttons, the shirt. Gone. She heard the metal click of a belt buckle, the teeth of a zipper, the scuff of a shoe, the soft *whoosh* of falling clothes.

Blood throbbing through her veins, her breathing already labored, she took a step back, and another, until she hit the warm, water-slick marble wall. Behind her, she reached for the faucet, flipped it on with one hand and both showerheads exploded into a pulsing rush of water that streamed over her body.

She closed her eyes, heard the shower door click closed, and felt the heat of Parker as he stood in front of her.

"Look at me," he commanded softly.

She did. His eyes were pure black with arousal, his jaw clenched, his nostrils flared with each ragged breath. Water matted his hair to his head and flattened the thatch of dark curls over the valleys and dips of his broad chest. With her eyes, she followed the water stream as it poured over the taut outline of his stomach and finally flowed over a daunting and mighty erection.

Without a word, he put one hand on either side of her head, caging her in without touching her.

"Anna." He mouthed her name, so softly she felt his breath on her face. "You have no idea how happy I am to know I can trust you."

She blinked into the water that streamed on her face. Why would he say that?

"Of course you can trust me," she said, her fingers curling against the wall as she fought the urge to scrape her hands over every inch of him.

"I just…wasn't sure."

The idea of Parker Garrison, man of certainty and decision, being unsure nearly buckled her knees. All her doubt disappeared with his admission; all her warnings vaporized in the steamy humidity of the shower.

"You can trust me," she repeated, closing her eyes and lifting her face. "And you can touch me."

At the command, he grazed a finger over her wet, parted lips, sliding the tip against her teeth, then following the watery path down her throat. She could hear him inhale with effort and strain as he glided over her breastbone and reached her nipple, making maddeningly slow circles around the peak.

"What else can I do, Anna?"

Her eyes remained closed as she let the silky, delicious touch of his finger send lightning through her. "You can kiss me."

He feathered her lips, so soft she wasn't sure it happened. She opened her mouth and his tongue flicked hers. Slow and steady and with remarkable control, he kissed her, while his other hand cupped her hip, caressing her wet skin, taking teasing strokes of the dips and curves of her backside.

"What else, Anna?" He inched closer so that every wet, hard, sculpted muscle of his body finally pressed against her. His thumb circled her nipple, torturing it to a hard nub as he rocked against her once, fully erect and wickedly hard.

She arched with a soft gasp, marble at her back, man at her front. "You can taste me."

With a groan of pleasure deep in his chest, he took his kisses lower, suckling her throat, licking her collarbone, then nibbling down to her breast. She twisted under his tongue, digging her fingers into his hair to guide his head from one breast to the other.

He gently squeezed both breasts, using his tongue to wipe water and flesh, then sucking each nipple with his eyes closed, as though it were the sweetest treat he'd ever enjoyed. She watched him, shaking, marveling, rolling as her insides twisted into an aching knot of pressure and pleasure.

"Parker," she moaned. "Please."

Straightening, he placed his knees between hers, easing her legs wider, opening her to him.

"What else can I do, Anna?" His voice was rough, with just a hint of tease and humor in the rasp.

He could do anything he wanted. Anything. Everything. And yet, the man who always had control gave her the power.

The thought made her dizzy as she flattened her hands over the soaking-wet hair on his chest, then slowly lowered them, loving every ripped muscle and the smooth flesh that covered them. Finally, she touched him, closing her hands over the velvet skin and sighing at how wonderfully shaped, how completely masculine he was.

She stroked him once and he grew even harder in her palms. She coiled her fingers around the length of him, considering all the things they could do to each other, but wanting only one.

She looked up at him, seeing him through the soft white clouds of steam, his expression intense, his eyes smoky.

"Make love to me, Parker."

The tiniest smile tugged at his mouth. "I thought you might say that," he said, reaching to a shelf above her head.

He tore the condom foil with ease and she took it from him, sliding it over him.

His eyes shuttered as he rose to meet her touch. Then his strong, sure hands gripped under her arms and pushed her up the slippery marble so he could enter her.

Just as he did, he covered her mouth with a ferocious kiss, thrusting his tongue and manhood inside her at exactly the same time, filling her completely.

Their delighted, desperate groans echoed off shower walls, rolled in the mist and gurgled with the water, both of them lost with each single-minded thrust of man against woman.

Shocked by the power of it, she wrapped her legs around his waist, locked her arms around his neck and rode him. Water blinded her now, so she buried her face in his shoulder, inhaling the smell of sex and soap and salt, her body coiling with achy pleasure.

Over and over, he ground out her name, pinning her to the wall, plunging as far into her as he could go, taking them both higher and higher to the unavoidable edge.

And finally she fell, digging her teeth into his skin, spiraling out of control and vaguely realizing that he was falling at the same time, filling her, needing her, loving her.

The steam clouds cleared as they slowly, carefully

slipped down the side of the shower to the floor, staying connected in that most intimate place as Anna remained on his lap, her legs like a vise around his waist.

The position brought them face-to-face, as he kissed her cheek, her neck, her eyes, her mouth, neither of them able to catch their breath.

"Whatever you do," he whispered, "don't even think about singing."

She laughed a little and dropped her forehead against his. "I can't sing."

"No kidding." He kissed her nose. "But you sure can make music."

She narrowed her eyes at him, joking aside. "I have to ask you a question."

"What's that?"

She reached up and twisted the faucet so that the water suddenly stopped. "When you came in here, you said something very strange. Why are you so surprised that you can trust me? That didn't have anything to do with…" She glanced down to where their bodies united. "This. Did it?"

"Actually," he said, his tone deliberate, his fingers winding through her wet hair. "It has everything to do with this. But I was referring to something else."

"What?"

"Let me take you home and hold you in my bed all night, Anna, then I'll tell you everything."

She nestled into him, warmed to the bone by the thought of spending the night with Parker. "Tell me everything about what?" she asked.

"About how I thought you were the spy in our company."

She stopped breathing just long enough to wonder if he noticed the goose bumps that rose despite the heat in the shower.

Eight

Every time Anna tried to form the words to tell him about her past, Parker kissed her.

As the wind whipped her hair in the convertible, he brushed the strands away at every stoplight and kissed her. While driving, he kept his hand on her leg, caressing and sliding up and down her thigh, sinfully intimate and completely possessive. There was no way she could speak coherently, let alone confess her life history.

And what would she say?

Parker, there's something you need to know about me....

No, that sounded as if she were guilty.

Funny thing you would have this corporate-spy problem...

There was nothing funny about it.

Before I spend the night making love to you...

No. No. She just didn't want to give up what she was about to experience. It was stupid, it was shortsighted and it was wrong.

But, she wanted a night with Parker Garrison so much she couldn't risk losing it.

Surely this conversation, this inevitable and uncomfortable conversation, would throw a bucket of cold water on their romance and then she'd never know the joy and pleasure of waking up in the arms of a man she…

Oh, Megan was right. She was in deep, undeniable…trouble.

"So, why'd you do it?" he asked as they reached the intersection at Ocean Drive.

Her throat closed, but she managed an even-toned response. "Why'd I do what?" *Let my manipulative boyfriend have access to my boss's computer and wreck my life?*

"Why'd you change your mind?" His fingers burned through the thin silk of her slacks and he rubbed her leg with his strong, large hand.

"Oh, that."

He laughed, removing his hand to shift gears, maneuvering through traffic, which was heavy, even for a weeknight. Then he slid her a slow, sexy grin and a sideways glance and resumed his private tour of her thigh.

"Yeah, *that*. Back there. In the shower. Big change of mind, don't you think?"

She tucked a still-damp, wind-tossed lock of hair behind her ear as they picked up speed.

She leaned her head back and closed her eyes in resignation. Why lie? "I've always been attracted to you."

"Really?" He actually sounded surprised. "Always?"

"Especially since I started working for you." She gave in to a smile, relieved to be admitting one truth, anyway. "I've fantasized about making love to you about a thousand times."

She felt him tap the brakes, so she opened her eyes to

see him staring at her, his jaw loose, his eyes wide. "Really? You mean, before London?"

She just nodded. "And since."

He shook his head, fighting a smile. "You sure hide it well. Along with everything else, I might add."

"I think getting involved with the CEO is not a wise career move."

He nodded. "I know you do. And you know I could help you get another job."

"I don't want another job," she said softly.

He slowed as they passed the stunning contemporary entrance to the Garrison Grand.

"You could work here," he suggested. "For my brother." Then he narrowed his eyes. "On second thought, you'd be safer working for Brooke or Brittany. Stephen would hit on you."

"I'm not interested in Stephen," she said. "Or working at the Garrison Grand." She glanced at the soaring, dramatic angles of the hotel, lit in pastel spotlights that bathed it in an ever-changing hue of art deco colors. "You'd still be the boss, in essence. You're still in charge of Garrison, Inc."

"Sort of," he said drily, accelerating into a hole in traffic and continuing north.

She should tell him. *Now.* "Parker…"

He turned to her, sneaked in another kiss on her cheek. "Let's make a deal for tonight, Anna. Let's forget you work for me, okay?" He nuzzled her neck for a moment as they stopped at a light. "Just for tonight, be my lover, not my administrative assistant. Let's forget everything keeping us apart and just be together."

The thrill of that danced through her again. His lover. Just for tonight. As for her big confession, couldn't it wait just one night?

Of course, she'd tell him in the professional atmosphere of the office. "But tomorrow—"

He cut her off with a nibble on her ear. "I'll take you home in the morning so you can change for work and we'll be back in the office by eight o'clock, just like always."

She closed her eyes. "But working together…it won't ever be the same."

"No, it won't," he agreed. "It'll be better."

"It'll be awkward."

"It'll be fine."

"It'll be obvious."

"It'll be fun."

She turned her face toward his and kissed him on the mouth. "You always get whatever you want, don't you?"

He grinned and twisted his finger around a tendril of her hair. "Usually, not always. And I want you. A lot. Tonight. Tomorrow." He tugged the hair gently and ignored the guy who honked when the light turned green. "I will make you feel very, very good, Anna. Trust me."

"I already feel very, very good," she assured him. Too good, she decided, to spoil the night with revelations about her past.

When he parked in an underground lot of the sky-high condo called the Tower, he teased her with more kisses. Somehow they made it to the elevator, where he backed her into the mirrored wall as it catapulted to the top floor.

"I live in the penthouse," he told her, toying with the top button of her blouse and pressing his body against hers, clearly ready to make love again. "So we have a minute now."

She laughed lightly, angling her head to give him access. "We need more than a minute."

He moaned softly as he slipped a hand over the lace cup of her bra. "You're right." He settled for a long, lazy kiss as the elevator soared, making Anna feel like the earth had dropped out from under her feet.

The car stopped and opened at the private entrance to the penthouse apartment. He unlocked one of the colossal double doors and led her into his world.

"God, this is amazing." She could barely take in the enormous space, all crisp lines and architectural angles, all shades of sand and coffee and wood, the walls no more than floor-to-ceiling plate glass with mind-bogglingly beautiful vistas of Biscayne Bay, barrier islands and a thousand dancing lights of the city of Miami.

"This is amazing," he repeated from behind her, closing his arms around her waist and pulling her into the granite of his body. "Amazing, beautiful, sexy." He glided his hands over her chest, burying his face in her hair, finding one spot of flesh on her neck to kiss.

She sighed and let him touch her, glorious sensations sliding from head to toe.

"Would you like a tour?" he asked. "A drink? Dinner?"

She turned to smile at him. "You cook?"

"I could scare up some spaghetti. Maybe a salad. Or have the chef at the Garrison Grand send over the special of the night." As though he couldn't possibly keep his hands off her, he pulled her back into him, kissing her forehead and then her nose. "Whatever you like."

She would pay for this procrastination. She would suffer when she had to sit across that desk and tell him that she hadn't been totally honest. She might even lose her job. But suddenly no price was too high for what she craved.

"What I like," she admitted softly, "is you."

His grin was slow and rich with satisfaction. "I like you, too." Then he scooped her up, kissed her on the mouth and carried her farther into the apartment.

* * *

"This wasn't nearly enough," Parker announced as he stole one more kiss outside the one-story Spanish-style bungalow in Coral Gables, the morning sun already burning the leather seats of his car. "While you're changing, why don't you pack a bag for tonight and we'll go out to dinner after work and then…"

Her smile evaporated as she opened the passenger door. "We'll see about tonight. We have to get through today first."

He climbed out, jogging around the front of his car to snag her at the first step of her front porch. "And that isn't going to be easy," he said.

She gave him a quizzical look. "Why not?"

"Because every time I see you, I'm going to want to take another shower." He pulled her in and kissed her. Damn, he couldn't get enough of that mouth.

"See?" She inched away, refusing the kiss. "I told you."

"I can handle a little distraction," he assured her. "Speaking of distraction, can I come in and watch you change?"

She chuckled, then pulled a set of keys from her handbag and stepped up to the patio covered with potted plants and two little wooden chairs.

"Sorry, we don't have time. The executive committee meeting starts in less than an hour." She unlocked the door and gave him a quick smile. "I'll just be five minutes since I already showered."

He grinned at the memory. "I know you're clean," he said as they entered the house. "I washed you myself."

"And so thoroughly," she quipped, sweeping an arm toward the small but cheery living room. "Not exactly the penthouse, but I call it home."

The little room was brightened by sliding glass doors that led to a cozy, plant-filled patio. Comfortable, tropical-print furniture and bright peach walls were bathed in sunshine all on a gleaming tile floor.

"I like your house," he said. It was inviting and unpretentious—just like Anna.

"Stay here, or in the kitchen," she said, a playful warning in her eyes. "You are not invited to my bedroom."

"I'll get there eventually," he said, releasing her hand.

"We'll see." Then she disappeared into the hallway.

She'd already changed this morning, he mused as he rounded the corner and found a sun-washed kitchen full of flowering plants, white cabinets and glossy butcher-block countertops.

She'd already started to pull away, mentally preparing for the workday that they would share. Could they do this? he wondered as he pulled out a ladder-back chair and sat at the table. Could they work together during the day and play together at night?

He'd never had a full-blown relationship with a woman at work. He fingered a fresh hibiscus floating in a bowl, taking a deep breath of the floral fragrance. But he'd never met anyone like Anna. She was smart and competent and wonderful at work…and sexy and giving and satisfying at play.

Could they have both?

What would happen if things didn't work out? Could they keep working together? And what would happen to her when it got out that she was dating—sleeping with—the CEO? Was it fair to her?

The thought of *not* being with her again squeezed his chest. They'd made love at least three times, and still, he wanted more. He woke up with her slender woman's body in his arms and all he wanted was…to do the same thing tomorrow. And the next day.

He felt better than he had in weeks. Better than he had

since his father had died, and certainly better than he had when he'd learned that Cassie Sinclair was his new sister and partner. Anna made the darkness disappear and it wasn't just her body. That was only the package for something truly…beautiful.

He heard the click of heels on tile and looked up to see her enter the kitchen.

"I see my administrative assistant has returned." He couldn't keep the disappointment out of his voice.

She brushed a self-conscious hand over the tan suit she wore over a simple, high-collared sweater loose enough that it didn't reveal what he knew to be luscious curves.

"It's going to be a busy day," she said, as though that explained her plain-Jane wardrobe.

And just like that, the playful, provocative lover disappeared and the professional, pragmatic assistant took her place. Why?

It was almost as if she was hiding something again.

Out of deference to her neatly styled hair, he put the top up as they drove back to downtown Miami. She held her hands on her lap and he filled the awkward silence with some music until they arrived and parked the car.

"I'll be up in a minute," she said.

"Where are you going?"

"I have to get something from my car. It's parked over there."

He understood. She didn't want to walk in with him. Someone in the office might put two and two together and the rumors would fly. Only they wouldn't be rumors. They'd be real. "Okay."

"Oh!" Suddenly a hand flew to her mouth and she gasped. "Parker, I forgot to do the spreadsheets for the meeting this morning. I'm so sor—"

"No problem. We don't need them."

She frowned at him. "What do you mean you don't need them?"

"I can't believe we were so involved last night that I never told you why I came back to the office." He reached to trace his finger along the line of her jaw and under her lower lip to remind her what had them so busy.

She paled slightly. "Why?"

"Not now. I don't want one of my brothers or sisters to beat me to my office. I'll tell you tonight. Over dinner. I promise." He stepped forward and took one more quick kiss. "See you in the office, sweetheart."

Without waiting for her to respond, he hustled to the elevator and didn't realize he was whistling until the doors opened and he found Stephen standing in the hallway outside of Garrison, Inc.

"If I didn't know you better," Stephen said without preamble, "I would accuse you of whistling something sounding suspiciously like…a show tune."

Parker laughed, but didn't deny it as he glanced at the darkened reception area. "No one is here yet?"

"Your front office is usually more efficient," Stephen noted.

Parker pulled out his keys and unlocked the lobby door. "Usually," he said. "But my assistant was busy."

"Busy stealing corporate secrets," Stephen said. "So now we check the computer program to see what your little spy did last night."

"We can," Parker said, hitting light switches as he headed down the hall. "But we won't find anything. I already checked."

"When?"

"I came back last night." He slid another key into his

office door, but it turned before he actually unlocked it. That was funny. It was always locked. Well, he had been pretty distracted after the shower. "Anna is not the spy."

"Are you sure?"

"Yep. She's a lot of things…" None of which he was about to share with his brother. "But she's no spy."

Stephen, however, went straight to the computer and started typing. "So you came back here, but you left the computer on?"

He must have. Damn, that woman had shut down his brain. "Yeah, but I checked it before…" *Before I found her in the shower.* "Before she left."

"Then she must have come back." Stephen's tone was ominous.

"What? No, she didn't. I know that she didn't."

"You're wrong," he said firmly, clicking at the newly installed program. "The bait is gone, bro. Eaten up and swallowed. And e-mailed to…" He clicked a few more keys. "An address of jjefferies@jefferiesbros.com." Stephen stood straight and leveled a hard-eyed gaze at his brother. "We nailed her."

"No." Parker strode toward the screen, trying to make sense of it. "I know that wasn't there last night when I got here. I checked. She was still here."

"Maybe she came back. The office door was unlocked and the computer was on. Would you have left it that way?"

In the state he'd been in? "I might have."

Stephen gave the desk a hard tap. "You have to fire her the minute she gets in."

"No!" Parker insisted. "It wasn't her."

"What's the matter with you?" Stephen growled. "She's the only person who has access to this office, you set up the bait, she ate it and now you fire her."

"I know she didn't come back here last night."

Stephen blew out a disgusted breath. "Unless you were with her all night, bro, you can't be sure of anything."

"I was. All night. Every minute. We left together around eight and we never separated until five minutes ago when I left her in the parking garage."

"Oh." Stephen notched a knowing eyebrow. "I see."

No, he didn't. Parker bit back the urge to correct his brother's impression that this was some kind of illicit office affair. But how? It was an affair; they did work in the same office and what they'd done in that shower definitely qualified as illicit.

"Someone else came in here after we left," he said.

Stephen looked dubious. "Are you positive? Maybe when you checked this last night you missed something. You've never run the program. You might have done something wrong."

"What time did that e-mail get sent?"

Stephen shook his head. "It doesn't say. It only tracks the physical keystrokes, not the time. But I suppose a decent hacker could figure it out. A good P.I., maybe."

"Then I'll hire one."

"And what if he figures out that your new girlfriend is guilty as hell?"

"She's not," he said, not even bothering to correct Stephen's phrasing. Anna *could* be his girlfriend. He'd be lucky to have her.

"But what if you weren't thinking with the right part of your body last night and you thought she hadn't touched your computer, but she had? What then?"

Parker suddenly felt like punching his brother in the smug, superior face. "I'll hire an investigator. She's not the spy, Stephen. I will prove it to you. If there's so much as a traffic ticket in Anna Cross's background, I'll fire her instantly."

Behind him, his office door creaked and Anna cleared her throat. "The executive committee is here, Mr. Garrison."

"She has access to everything," Stephen said in a harsh whisper as she closed the door. "Including the boss. You'd better know what you're doing, Parker."

Had he really checked that computer thoroughly, or had the shower distracted him? He let out a low, slow breath. "I do," he said confidently.

But just in case, he called the company investigator before he went into the exec committee.

Nine

If there's so much as a traffic ticket in Anna Cross's background, I'll fire her instantly.

The words reverberated in Anna's ears all morning long, while the phone rang and packages were delivered and e-mail was sent and received. Life went on…around her. Inside, turmoil raged.

She had no idea what had compelled Parker to make the comment that she'd overheard as she'd opened his door. But it left her with one choice: to tell him the truth before he figured it out.

But that option had a downside that made her whole body ache. She'd lose him. Not that she actually *had* him. But, last night, when they'd made love, she'd felt something so real and powerful. Was that just incredible sex? She didn't know yet, but she wanted to find out. She wanted to find out with every fiber of her being.

But if she told him that her former boyfriend had used

her computer password to access proprietary files—her boss's proprietary files—and that she'd taken a job with Garrison, Inc. without ever revealing that, she'd never get the chance to make love to him again. Parker, she knew, put business before anything personal. Always.

But if she didn't tell him, then their whole relationship was built on a lie. And that was just as bad as losing him.

Wasn't it?

At eleven-thirty, her phone rang and the sound of Megan Simmons's voice rang like real music in Anna's ears. When Megan said she was in Miami for the day for another conversation about the possible partnership, Anna seized the opportunity.

"Please have lunch with me," she begged. "I need to talk to you."

"Are you all right?" Megan asked, concern in her voice.

Anna closed her eyes. *All right* was relative. "I just need to talk to someone who can give me some advice."

"I'm in SoBe," Megan said. "I have a sliver of time until I have to get to an early-afternoon meeting and I was just going to grab a sandwich. Can you meet me at the News Café in about fifteen minutes?"

Anna was already opening her drawer to grab her purse. "Let me turn my calls over to the receptionist and I'll be there as fast as I can."

The trendy outdoor restaurant was teeming with tourists and locals, but Megan had somehow snagged a table right along the sidewalk of Ocean Drive. She was sipping an iced tea by the time Anna arrived.

Before the waiter brought Anna's bottled water, she spilled the whole story of what she'd overheard that morning, keeping out some very important parts...like what she'd done the night before.

"What should I do?" she asked Megan when she'd finished, breathless. "Should I preempt the inevitable or take a chance?"

"You slept with him, didn't you?"

So much for keeping secrets from Megan. "I hadn't planned to tell you that part."

"Why not? It's all over your face, literally and figuratively. Your glowing with satisfaction and…" Megan reached forward and touched Anna's chin lightly. "I believe I see a little beard burn there."

Lying wasn't an option. "I spent the night with him," Anna admitted.

"And that's why this is a dilemma," Megan said thoughtfully. "Because now it's more than a job. Now it's sex."

"It wasn't just sex," she said quietly.

"It never is, to the woman."

Megan sounded like the voice of experience and, as always, Anna had to fight the urge to ask her just what that experience was. Obviously, it had resulted in Jade. But today's impromptu lunch certainly wasn't the time or place.

"The question is," Anna said, "should I tell him about what happened to me in Indiana? If I do, we could both be in trouble. You knew about the accusations against me when you recommended me for the job."

Megan waved her hand. "I'm not scared of Garrisons," she said, "and neither should you be."

"I'm not scared of him," Anna replied. "I'm…crazy about him."

"Oh, Anna," Megan half moaned and shook her head. "Be careful. Men like that, oh, I don't have to tell you. Michael Montgomery was the same way. Controlling. Arrogant. Demanding."

"Parker's not any of those things. And he's not Michael Montgomery, who was a snake and a cheat and a jerk."

Megan snorted softly. "He's a Garrison. So he's all of those things."

"Really, Meg, not deep down inside. When we made love, he was very giving, very gentle. He let me call the shots, gave me every opportunity to say no or at least be sure I knew what I was doing."

Megan dropped her elbows on the table. "Three words, my friend. Run, don't walk." At Anna's look, she added, "You asked for my advice. You don't have to like it, but that's what I'm telling you to do."

"I have another idea," Anna said slowly. "What do you think if I tried to find the real culprit and then told Parker about my background?"

Megan leaned back as the waiter delivered sandwiches. When he was gone, she said, "Okay, let's play with this. That might solve all your problems, and some of Parker's. How could you do it?"

"It would take some sleuthing, but I do have four years' experience in human resources. I know how to interpret a personnel file."

"You could go through phone logs for calls to or from the Jefferies Group," Megan suggested. "Or you could find out who in the company has ever worked for them."

"Although I imagine he's already done all of that," Anna said, picking up a quarter of a sandwich as the idea took hold. "But maybe I could see something he hasn't."

"Anna, shouldn't he just believe you?" Megan insisted. "I mean, if you have any kind of connection or relationship?"

"In a perfect world, yes," Anna agreed. "But we live in an imperfect one. And the fact that my ex-boyfriend stole my password and accessed my boss's files and the fact that my ex-boyfriend also happened to be my boss's biggest rival and the newspapers and company accused me.... Well, it would be very hard for him not to see a pattern."

"*Wrongly* accused you," Megan corrected.

"It still doesn't look good. Even four years later." How long would she be running from that past?

While they ate, Megan told Anna a little bit about her morning interview and how close she was to taking the new job. But by the time the check arrived, the conversation drifted back to Anna's plan.

"Can you get access to some of that information? The phone logs or background checks? From some of your contacts in HR, maybe?"

"Maybe," Anna said. "I'd have to do it quickly. Today."

"Hey." Megan reached across the table and took Anna's hand. "I know you don't want to hear this, but he's just another guy, you know."

"No, he's not," Anna argued. "And I really, really like him. I wouldn't have slept with him if I didn't. I haven't been with anyone else since Michael—"

"Another alpha dog," Megan interjected.

"Parker's not like he appears on the outside, Megan. He's in charge, yes, but he's also, I don't know, vulnerable."

Megan raised her eyebrow in warning. "So are you, Anna." Then she checked her watch and squashed a tiny shriek. "Oh, no. I have to be in my next meeting in twelve minutes."

"Go," Anna said, shooing her with the check in hand. "This is on me. Thanks for listening, Megan."

Megan was already standing and pulling her purse onto her shoulder. "Thanks for lunch. Good luck with your secret investigation. I still think you should run." She blew a kiss. "And I'd better do just that. Bye." She disappeared into the restaurant.

As Anna scanned the restaurant for their waiter, her gaze drifted across the street to a group of pedestrians, where one very tall, dark-haired man stood out.

Stephen Garrison crossed Ocean Drive with determination and confidence, a cell phone pressed to his ear. As he flipped it closed with his chin, he caught her eye.

She nodded in acknowledgment. "I take it the meeting is finally over," she said as he reached her table.

"It is," he said, glancing at the empty seat with a half-eaten sandwich across from her. "Lunching with a Garrison employee, Miss Cross?"

She swallowed at the unmistakable doubt in his voice. The same doubt she'd hear from Parker when she told him about what happened in Indiana. She thought about defending herself, mentioning that she was with Megan, whom he might remember from when she had done work for the Garrisons, but she just shrugged. She'd save her defense for the brother who mattered.

"Just a friend," she said.

He looked around. "Where is he?"

She shifted in her seat. "*She* just left."

"Oh, I see." He gave her a tight smile. "I'd better get back to the hotel. Goodbye."

"Bye." The word stuck in her throat as she watched him walk away, so much like his brother. So much like the man she'd slept with the night before. So much like the man she didn't want to lose.

Should she run? Or try to vindicate herself? She had nothing to lose…but Parker.

Her cell phone vibrated and the caller ID read the main

number for Garrison, Inc., sending little waves of guilt and worry over Anna. "Hello?"

"It's Sheila McKay."

"Is something wrong, Sheila?"

"You tell me," she said with a dry laugh. "Mr. G. just blew out of here when the exec committee meeting ended, said he had an appointment."

She tried to visualize his calendar, which she'd swear had been open that afternoon. "Okay. Does he need me?"

"Not during the day, apparently." Sheila's voice was rich with insinuation. "But he said to tell you he'd meet you at seven tonight at the Opalesce Room in the Garrison Grand."

Her heart rolled around like a tumbleweed. "All right."

Sheila laughed. "Whatever you told him, it must have worked, honey."

"I'm sure he wants to go over business," Anna said, copping her most professional voice.

"Yeah, I'm sure. In the private dining room. I just reserved it for you."

"So he's not coming back for the afternoon?" Anna asked.

"I don't think so."

"All right. Thanks."

She had one chance to make Parker believe and trust her. Could she find out anything in one afternoon?

Parker crossed and uncrossed his ankles impatiently, glancing around the high-end, upscale Miami office. Too bad the slightly stoop-shouldered, thin-haired investigator with the spot-on name of Ace Martin didn't have a chipped Formica desk with a green-shaded lamp. Then he'd be right out of central casting for a B movie called *Ace Martin: P.I.*

But Ace ran an elegant shop, complete with a good-looking receptionist and a few staff members dressed well enough to let Parker know Martin Securities was making a few bucks. Garrison, Inc. had been contributing to Ace's bank account for years.

But this job didn't fall under Garrison, Inc. Parker had asked Ace to investigate Anna Cross on the Q.T. And the urgent call from Ace that had come in at noon left Parker no doubt that something had been uncovered.

"Sorry to keep you waiting, Parker," Ace said as he ambled into the room, his hands full of files and paper. He dropped it all on his desk to give Parker a hearty handshake. "I'm glad you could come over. I didn't want to take all this into your office. Not with our culprit right there."

Parker's stomach dropped. "So you've got bad news on Anna, huh?"

Ace's expression tightened as he went around his desk to sit across from Parker. "I'm afraid so."

He almost swore. He didn't want Anna to be guilty. He wanted her to be… Hell, he just wanted her. And now, he'd never have her. "What have you got? How tight is the connection to Jefferies?"

"I have no idea. I couldn't find one."

Parker gave the other man a sharp look. "Then what's wrong?"

"What's wrong is that your AA has quite a history. Are you aware that you're not the first CEO she's worked for?"

He knew so little about her. Had he even seen her résumé when the director of HR had recommended her for the job as his assistant? Probably not.

"She's been at Garrison, Inc. for four years," he said, unable to deny the little hope and defensiveness in his voice.

"Before that she was the administrative assistant to a gentleman by the name of Barry Lynch, the president and

CEO of a midsize tech firm in Indiana called FiberTech. They make fiber optic cables and such."

A little wisp of jealousy twirled around him. Had Anna showered in Barry Lynch's private bath, too? "And?"

"And she was fired for spying."

This time, he couldn't repress the curse that bubbled up.

Ace agreed with a nod. "Seems she had a very personal and intimate relationship with—"

"Stop." Parker held his hand up, swallowing the sour taste that suddenly filled his mouth. "I don't need the details of how she slept with her boss."

"Not her boss," Ace said, turning a photocopy of a newspaper article around and sliding it across the desk to Parker. "Her boss's biggest rival. A venture capitalist named Michael Montgomery who sat on the board of a competitive company. She dated him for, oh, about a year. Very high-profile guy, wealthy and successful."

At least she was consistent. He glanced at the paper, his gaze darting over a black-and-white picture of Anna with shorter hair. The headline blared Local Secretary Steals Secrets.

"According to that article," Ace continued, "she used her access to spoon-feed highly confidential information to the competitor, which was a company where her boyfriend had about twenty percent of the stock."

Parker flinched as if he'd been punched. History sure did have a way of repeating itself. "What kind of information?"

"The usual. New product launch dates, marketing strategies and new R & D efforts. The implication from this reporter is that she was getting some financial kickbacks."

"Implication? Was anything proven?"

"Actually the charges were dropped by the Fiber-Tech CEO."

Hope curled its sticky fingers around his heart. "Then she wasn't guilty?"

Ace rolled his eyes. "She worked a deal, I'm sure. The boyfriend was kicked off the board of the competing company, and left town. She was fired and moved to Miami about two weeks later. You'll notice that her résumé on file with Garrison makes no mention of the job at FiberTech. And, Parker, if she wasn't guilty, why didn't they run a follow-up story?"

And, worse, why didn't she tell him? She had to know that if this came out, she'd be under suspicion. Why hadn't she told him—in London, the night they'd spent together, all this time they'd been working together?

Because she was doing the same thing again. It was her scam. Maybe being in the bathroom where he could get his first glimpse of her was all part of it, to get closer, to get better information during pillow talk.

His temples throbbed as he reached for the papers. Computer printouts detailed the information she'd given to the competitor. A few pictures of her at social events on the arm of a tall, jet-setting type.

"You can keep all that," Ace said, sliding it into a manila file folder. "Wish I had better news, Parker."

"Hey, we solved a very big problem for Garrison today." Parker took the folder, tapping all the papers together with a sharp rap as he stood. "But send me the bill."

"This one's on the house," Ace said. "Didn't take me but half an hour to get all this off the Internet. I'm surprised she even got the job in the first place at Garrison."

Parker's smile was strained. "She can be pretty charming."

Ace nodded knowingly. "It's obvious she charmed you."

"Is it?" He laughed lightly. "I hate to be transparent."

"Nah, it's my job to read people. If you didn't care about her, you wouldn't be so miserable to hear the truth. You'd just fire her and move on. Which, knowing you, is what you'll do. Business will always trump personal feelings for you, Parker. That's why your dad left you in charge."

Sort of left him in charge. Somehow, in the space of a few weeks, Parker's whole foundation had crumbled. He shook Ace's hand, and barely smiled at the pretty receptionist who called, "Goodbye," and waved pink-tipped fingers at him.

With the top down and music up, Parker cruised through the streets of South Miami and barely noticed the traffic on U.S. 1. In his mind's eye, all he could see was Anna, laughing. Anna, sighing. Anna, wet and wild and wanton in the shower.

Was that all an act to get information?

Something deep inside of him screamed *no*.

He recognized that voice. That was his gut calling, and he usually didn't ignore it. On an impulse, he whipped a left turn and instead of heading home to stew, he barreled the BMW toward Garrison, Inc. He had to know the truth. He *had* to.

If it was bad, he'd fire her and forget her, just as Ace Martin had predicted. But if she could possibly convince him that everything in that file was wrong…

He threw a quick glance at the manila folder on the passenger seat, held in place by his leather briefcase. Damning evidence, all of it. But it all rang untrue to him.

It all rang untrue to a blind man in…lust. Or, worse.

In record time, he parked and jogged to the elevator just as it arrived to take him directly to the twenty-second floor.

Sheila McKay's bright blue eyes widened as he yanked

the glass door open and stepped into Garrison, Inc. "Oh, Mr. Garrison, we didn't expect you back today."

All the more reason to show up. "Is Anna here?" he asked.

Sheila's heavily lined lips curled up. "You two ought to try calling each other. She keeps asking the same about you every time she flits in and out of here to copy files, all breathless like she's in such a big hurry. Guess she wants to get out of here early for your date. I made the reservations, by the way."

Parker's grasp tightened on the manila folder he held. Why was she copying files in a hurry? Why would she ask if he was coming back? The bad taste threatened to return to his mouth. He didn't respond to the receptionist's obvious ploy for gossip fodder, but headed straight through the arched doorway and down the hall toward Anna's desk.

He rounded the corner and froze. Her desk was empty and his door was closed. What was she doing in there?

Showering? God, he could only hope that was the worst of her employee infractions. Slowly, he walked to his office door. He turned the handle silently and opened the heavy cherrywood without making a single noise.

Her head bent over, her back to him, she clicked madly on his computer keys. There was no reason for her to be on his computer. None.

Soundlessly, he walked across the room, leaning a little to the right so he could see what was on the screen. She was so engrossed, she never even moved.

"Damn," she swore softly. "Why can't I find that password?"

All he could see was the Jefferies Group logo. Son of a bitch, that was enough.

"I changed the password."

With an audible gasp, she spun around, surprise and

shock widening her eyes, shame and horror darkening her cheeks.

"The new password is *liar*. That ought to be easy to remember, don't you think?"

"I'm not a liar," she said, forcing her chin up to meet his gaze.

He tossed a folder at her and a dozen papers fluttered around like feathers around her lap and the floor. "Omission counts as a lie, Anna."

She dragged her gaze from his burning brown eyes to the first piece of paper on the floor at her feet. Then she just closed her eyes, placed her hands on the armrest and dug her fingers into the leather. "Will you give me an opportunity to explain?"

"I wanted to," he said, hating that emotion made his voice catch. Steeling himself, he looked over her shoulder at the computer screen. "Until I saw that."

She opened her mouth, then snapped it shut as she stood, visibly shaken. "I knew this would happen. You won't even listen to me. That's why I haven't told you."

He just stared at her, his brain at war with a body that wanted all the papers to disappear and all the lies to disintegrate.

"Do you believe everything you read?" she demanded.

"I believe you are a very cunning woman."

"Parker, please, I—" She reached her hands up, maybe in a helpless gesture, maybe to touch him, but he backed away before she burned him with so much as a fingertip.

He had no control where she was concerned. For some reason, she got to him. If she touched him or kissed him, the next thing he knew, he'd be listening to her. Believing her.

That couldn't be good for his business. That couldn't be good for him.

"I want you to leave," he said quietly.

Her eyes flashed. "You're firing me?"

"Just leave, Anna. And don't take a single thing with you."

The color that had deepened her cheeks drained, leaving nothing but pale, alabaster shock. "You're firing me." This time it wasn't a question.

"Yes."

"Before you give me a chance to even tell you my side."

"Your side," he said, "is the competition. Why don't you call Jordan or Emilio? Maybe they need an administrative assistant."

She drew back as if she'd been slapped, and guilt sucker punched his stomach, along with the sudden need to hold her and take back the words.

"I won't press charges," he said, stepping back to give her a wide berth. The words and the gesture felt foreign and wrong, but he forced himself to continue. "I'll have Sheila escort you."

She narrowed her eyes at him. "That won't be necessary. I know how to leave a building after I've been terminated."

I bet you do. Something inside him kept him from saying the sarcastic remark out loud.

She walked across the office, and he followed her, keeping the door open so he could see her desk. As she slid open her bottom drawer to get her handbag, he pulled out his cell phone, hit one number and Stephen answered on the first ring.

"Mystery solved," he said.

She pivoted and gave him a sharp, disbelieving look.

"Well done," Stephen said. "Let's celebrate."

He didn't feel very celebratory. "Sure. Meet me at Estate tonight."

Without another word, Anna strode down the hall, head held high, shoulders back, chin in the air. Not at all, Parker thought, the way a guilty woman would slink from the scene of the crime.

"You sure you nailed her?" Stephen said in his ear.

Hell, no. "Yeah."

"I knew you'd do it. I knew you'd make the right choice when it came to the company."

The right choice? This felt anything but *right*.

Ten

The water was as hot as her old Coral Gables plumbing could muster, but it still didn't wash away the sickening sensation of déjà vu.

Anna leaned her head back, lifted her face directly to the stinging spray and flattened her hands on the grouted tile wall.

Oh, yeah. Been here. Done this. Felt this agony.

Water spritzed into her parted lips, over her eyelids, down her cheeks. Not that there were tears to wash away, she thought bitterly. She hadn't even cried once and it was almost ten o'clock.

This time, she was just mad.

All she could see was Parker's torn and pained expression, and all she could feel was the impact of being on the wrong side of that one-of-a-kind focus.

She twisted the knobs and shut off the water, the pipes clanging with the sudden change in pressure. That was usually her final note to a song. But she had no song in her head or her heart. They were too full of regret and disgust.

"Now what?" she said to herself, climbing out of the shower and wrapping herself in a terry robe. "Let's see, Anna, last time you packed up and ran like a scared kitten. Where will you go this time?"

Her voice was bitter and sarcastic as she wiped steam from the mirror with a quick swipe of her sleeve, revealing her own ravaged expression, her lusterless gaze, her sad, sad pallor. She looked like the victim of circumstance she was.

Victim.

"That's a bad word, Anna Cross," she whispered to her reflection. "Very bad."

The thing that stunned her the most was that Parker Garrison had never made her feel that way. He wasn't like Michael Montgomery in that regard. He wasn't like...anybody.

But was he worth fighting for?

The mirror fogged up almost instantly and this time, she used her palm, noisily rubbing against the glass to get a clear shot of herself.

"It doesn't matter if he is or he isn't," she said to herself. "But you are, Anna Cross. *You* are worth fighting for."

The realization was so strong and sudden and clear, it nearly lifted her up on her toes. Why would she just let him win? He was dead wrong. He would figure that out as soon as the next corporate leak occurred.

And then what? He'd come skulking back for more shower sex? No. No. *No.*

But what could she do? Take him on? Deny? Slap him in the face until he listened to her?

Oh, she could waltz up to him at the nightclub where

he was tonight, knocking back drinks with his brother, high-fiving each other on their success in sniffing out the spy.

Yeah, she could march right up to the Great and Powerful Parker Garrison and tell him off. The idea was so absurd, it actually made her smile for the first time all day.

She wandered into her bedroom and headed for the closet, letting the little fantasy take flight. If she would do something like that—just *if*—what would she wear? She stared at the offerings. A gray business suit. A beige shapeless dress. A brown ensemble perfect for…

Hiding.

She'd been running and hiding for so long. Until Parker had seen underneath her gray-and-brown shields. Literally, at first. But then, she'd stopped hiding from him. And it had felt so damn good…until now.

With a soft grunt, she shoved a handful of hangers to the left. Again and again, she pushed her clothes as far to one side as she could squeeze them.

And then she saw the red gown she'd worn in London. She eased it over the rack, and behind that… Oh.

Her fingers closed over the straps of a pure white sheath that fit like a dream and moved as if it were part of her body. She lifted the hanger and smiled at the memory of how much she used to like to wear this sexy, splendid dress.

She held it up and turned to the full-length mirror on the inside of the closet door, taking a little breath when she saw the reflection.

No woman could hide in this dress. In fact, she would jump out and demand attention. Demand that someone listen to her.

A woman could make a point in this dress, she thought.

And when she was done making that point, a woman could make a man suffer just by walking away.

Lovingly, she laid the silky fabric on the bed and, like magic, a song started playing in her head.

Humming softly, she settled into the chair at her vanity, opened up a drawer full of makeup and creams and lined a few up.

She was done hiding and running and worrying and hoping no one knew who she was or what had happened to her. She was done having fantasies fill her brain. She was done letting powerful men make wrong assumptions and wreck her life and break her heart.

By the time she locked her front door and walked to the car, her stilettos were keeping perfect time to her favorite song from *West Side Story*.

Yep, she felt pretty. Pretty strong. Pretty brave. Pretty smart. Much too smart to make the same mistake twice.

The natives were getting restless at Estate and it was only midnight. The DJ had pumped up the beat; the beautiful people were blissed out on strategically situated sofas; the curved, high-tech bars at every corner were three deep with drinkers of pastel-colored martinis and straight shots of dark amber courage. Adam's state-of-the-art mood lighting shifted almost imperceptibly from pink to blue to white and red, washing the Venetian glass mirrors and crystal chandeliers in unearthly colors.

Parker leaned into the cushiony leather of a corner alcove tucked into a towering keystone arch, the Lucite table between him and Stephen empty but for two beers and one PDA/cell phone combination.

The cell phone that didn't ring. Instead, its very presence just teased Parker with the temptation to make just one call. So far, he managed to ignore that temptation.

From where they sat, Parker had a clear shot of most of the lounge and a few of the six different bars, as well as the sweeping staircase that led to this, the lowest and most private level in the forty-thousand-square-foot club.

"You haven't said five words since we got here." Stephen nudged his brother's beer glass with his. "You gotta get over it, man."

Parker swallowed, his gaze moving across the slithering, achingly hip crowd, the heavy mix of perfume and booze and lingering incense as thick as the desperation to look cool.

"I'm over her," he assured his brother, taking a swig of whatever exotic ale Adam had sent to their table. "Trust me, I am so over her."

Stephen laughed. "Actually, I said get over *it*. Not *her*."

"She is it," Parker said softly. "I mean, she is the problem," he added quickly. "Now I have to hire a new AA, I have to figure out what information she leaked, I have to—"

"Lick your wounds."

"I'm not wounded," he insisted. Not much, anyway.

Stephen reached for the PDA. "Come on. Call that model. What was her name?"

"Yvette. Yvonne. I don't remember."

"It'll be in here." Stephen pressed a button and Parker yanked the device from his hands.

"Chill out. I don't want to call her."

"What about that cute little redhead who did the brochure? Weren't you going to ask her out?"

Parker glared at his brother. "Do you actually think I'm going to pick up my phone and hit on another woman right now?"

"Okay, forget the phone." Stephen cocked his head

toward one of the bars. "The brunette in the ass-hugging black skirt has been telegraphing interest since we sat down."

Parker didn't look. "No, thanks."

"Aah, man."

"What? What are you ah-manning about?"

"Come on, Parker. You were with Anna once? Twice? It's not like it mattered. She screwed you, in bed and out of it."

Parker clenched his fist, then relaxed it. He'd be saying the same thing to Stephen if the situation were reversed. "I've known her for three months, Stephen. We built a rapport working together. The sex was just...just..."

"Just sex."

"Not even close." Parker looked out at the sea of people, at the few new ones who ventured down the long red-carpeted staircase. "It was more than that."

"I see," Stephen said.

"No, you don't."

"Actually, I do."

The wry tone in Stephen's voice took Parker by surprise. "What do you mean?"

"I mean..." Stephen lifted his beer, but didn't drink. "The one that got away. It sucks. Big-time."

Parker inched back, looking at his brother in a new light. "Is this the voice of experience?"

Stephen took a drink, his own gaze shifting away, his lack of a response speaking volumes. "Whoa, look at *that*."

"I just told you, Stephen," Parker said, fiddling with his PDA. "I'm not interested."

"You'll be interested in this."

He pressed the button, giving voice to the thought that had been reverberating in his brain for the last two hours. "I think I should call Anna."

"No need," Stephen said.

"Just to see if, you know…" He'd been pretty rough on her. "She's okay."

"Oh, she's fine. Trust me."

"I think I'll call her." He punched in her home number.

"You won't get an answer," Stephen said.

Parker put the phone to his ear. "How do you know that?"

"Because unless I'm mistaken, that vision in white is Anna Cross."

Parker jerked around, his attention drawn like a magnet to the stairs. His jaw unhinged. His eyes widened. His breath caught.

And his heart damn near stopped. "Anna?" he managed to whisper.

Just then, she turned, and the impact of her beautifully made-up face and the intensity of her jade-green gaze slammed his heart back into action. Dark hair cascaded over her bare shoulders, stark against the creamy-white dress. A dress that fit like snakeskin and ended midthigh, showing off those stupefyingly perfect legs.

The PDA hit the Lucite with a clunk and Stephen leaned back and laughed. "This actually might be fun to watch."

"You don't need to be here, Stephen," Parker said with clenched teeth.

"Hey," Stephen said. "She's the enemy. You need back-up."

"I don't need anything." Except *that*.

She strode like a white cat, her tilted eyes locked on him, her expression leaving no doubt that her arrival at Estate was no coincidence. The woman was on a mission.

The crowd parted to let her through and Parker's gut grew tighter with each long step she took, fire whipping through his body as he watched her. Along with every single man in the club.

She stopped as she reached the alcove of their table, no smile even threatening. Parker couldn't help it. His gaze dropped and lingered over every curve and cut of her body.

Hitching one hand on her hip, she jutted her chin as though she knew exactly how incredible she looked.

"What are you doing here?" Stephen asked. "Spying?"

"Stephen," Parker said, his attention still on Anna. "I'll handle this."

"No," she said, her voice low. "*I'll* handle this." She placed her fingertips on the table, and leaned just enough to draw his eyes back to the low neckline of her dress and the rise of her breasts.

She wasn't wearing a bra.

His throat went dry and he cleared it, forcing himself to pin her with a glare that would leave no doubt who had more power in this situation. Even if she was towering over him in her high heels, and he was…

Hard as the Lucite table that separated them.

Damn her.

"Mr. Garrison." She almost spat the name. "We haven't finished our conversation."

Stephen started to say something, but Parker held up his hand. "Let her finish or leave us alone."

Stephen didn't move, and Anna drew in a slow, steady breath and stared at Parker. "I am not the corporate spy you are looking for. I don't care whether you believe me or not, because the fact that I am telling the truth will be clear soon enough. Whoever it is—I was trying to find out when you snuck up on me today—"

"I didn't—"

She silenced him with tapered eyes. "Whoever it is," she continued, "will spy again and then you will realize you made a mistake."

"I'm willing to take that chance."

"I'm sure you are. But that's not why I'm here."

His control slipped a little, along with his gaze. "Then why are you here?" To prove she could reduce him to a desperate, sex-starved, lovesick teenager? It was working.

"To tell you that four years ago I was used by a man very much like you. My lover."

The word almost choked him.

"He oozed power and control and authority over everyone."

At that moment, Parker didn't feel very powerful, controlling or authoritative. He was simply mesmerized by the cool, confident woman in front of him.

"I had something he wanted and he took it from me."

"What was that?" he asked.

She smiled. "My password. He stole it, accessed my company's computers and left a trail that led directly and exclusively to me. When I was accused of the crime, he didn't come to my defense. When the newspapers covered the story, he didn't refute it. When I was terminated from my job, he didn't support me. But when the truth came out, as it always does, I was exonerated."

"Why doesn't my private investigator know that?"

"Because the charges were quietly dropped, and the story was no longer interesting and the damage was done, so I ran away without ever forcing the issue or demanding my name be cleared. I was scared and I ran."

"And got a job under false pretenses," he said, trying hard to make his voice sound stern but being totally betrayed by the overload of Anna on his senses.

"Where I spent the next four years as a stellar employee," she snapped back. "But then I made a huge mistake."

"Other than breaking into my computer?"

"I trusted you. I thought that a real heart beat in that steel case of yours. I thought that a real man lived in that chiseled body. I thought that when you were pushed against the wall, you might, you just might, put something and someone before your precious, almighty, profitable company."

He tried to swallow, but couldn't.

"You thought wrong," he said, hating the words the minute they were out. But what choice did he have? In front of his brother and half of Miami, he could hardly stand up, throw his arms around her and tell her she was *right*.

Even though that was exactly what he wanted to do.

She stood ramrod straight and crossed her arms, which made her seem more powerful and in control. And, God help him, sexy. "At my next job, I won't hide who I am, what I've done or where I've been. Because I have nothing to hide. Nothing to be ashamed of. Nothing. But you?" She arched an eyebrow and managed to deliver a boatload of sympathy, pity and disdain with that one muscle move. "That's a different story. Goodbye, Mr. Garrison."

She turned on one ice pick of a heel and walked straight ahead, her body swaying to the rhythm of Parker's thudding heart.

Next to him, Stephen took a long drink. "Think she's lying?"

The PDA buzzed a soft digital tone. Without taking his eyes from the white second skin that moved up the stairs, Parker answered it.

"Yes?"

"Mr. Garrison, my name in Barry Lynch. I'm the CEO of FiberTech in Indianapolis, Indiana."

Parker frowned at Stephen as he processed what he heard. "Go ahead," he said into the phone.

"I was contacted by a private investigator today and if I don't talk to you, I don't think I'm going to sleep tonight."

"What is it?"

He leaned back, closed his eyes and listened as the man talked. When he was finished, Parker clicked off and set the device down.

"No," he said to his brother. "She's not lying. And I just lost the best woman I ever had." He dropped his head into his hands and swore softly.

"Told you it sucks."

Parker lifted his head and looked at his brother. "I don't want to lose her."

Stephen shrugged. "You have to grovel. Apologize. Spend money. Or, embrace celibacy."

"I'm serious. I have to…" *Tell her what she means to me.* "I have to do something."

"I recognize that you are a man of action, Parker," Stephen said. "But I hate to tell you. You can do all that and more and I have a sneaking suspicion that woman is never going to talk to you again."

Parker scooped up the PDA and pushed himself off the cushy leather, already forming a plan, already anxious. "How do you know?"

"Voice of experience."

Eleven

Anna let herself into the dark, silent office without making a noise, her whole body still humming from the confrontation with Parker.

Not that the scene in Estate truly qualified as a *confrontation*. That implied that there were two sides in a discussion. She pretty much owned that round.

Smiling smugly, she turned off the office alarm and kicked off the sky-high heels that had been torturing her toes. They'd done their night's work. He'd all but drooled on his precious electronic gadget.

She glanced at Sheila's perfectly neat desk, half tempted to leave her a note. She hadn't explained this afternoon when she'd left and no doubt Sheila had gossiped about the boss's assistant-turned-girlfriend's sudden departure to everyone from Mario in the mail room on up.

No, it didn't matter. They weren't really friends and gossip couldn't hurt her anymore. She padded down the carpeted hall in bare feet, the silk of her dress cool on her skin. Running her hands through her hair, she practically skipped.

That had felt so good! And the look on his face—the absolute lust and pain and misery in his deep brown eyes—that had felt good, too. Hadn't it?

She paused as she reached her desk, considering that.

She hadn't really intended to hurt him. He was Parker Garrison, after all, and basically invincible. She just wanted the truth out. She hadn't expected that it would twist her heart to see him again, and shoot that fire through her whole body when he'd taken in her drop-dead white dress and had looked as if he might, well, drop dead.

With a soft sigh, she folded into her chair and opened the top drawer. She had personal items, pictures of her family in Indiana, some inexpensive jewelry, a few hair clips.

A suspense novel she'd been reading on her lunch hour and some personal files were in the bottom drawer. She scanned the area for a box or bag that she could put it all in, but didn't see anything. Maybe in the executive kitchen.

In the galley-shaped kitchen, she hit the overhead light and spied a small plastic container Mario used for mail. She picked it up, hit the light switch with her elbow and turned the corner to her desk.

And froze dead in her tracks at the sight of Parker Garrison leaning on her desk, dangling her sandals from one finger.

"You dropped something, Cinderella."

"They hurt."

"Yeah," he agreed. "They killed me."

She refused to react to the compliment. "Shower's in the back, Parker. Left knob's cold. I'm just getting my personal belongings. You're more than welcome to check everything I take out of here or call security to escort me. I'm not doing anything illegal, untoward or improper."

"The way you look in that dress could qualify for all three."

"Stop." She approached the desk, holding her breath that he would move so she could finish her task. "It won't work."

He reached out for her hand, but she jerked out of his touch.

"Anna. I'm sorry."

Her breath rushed out and she cursed herself for it. "It's too late, Parker."

"I mean it," he said. "I'm sorry."

"And I'm sure that pains you to say," she volleyed back. "But if you want forgiveness, you're not going to get it."

"Will you stay?"

She choked a laugh. "No."

"Will you stay at the company?"

"No."

"Will you stay in Miami?"

"No."

This time he sighed, the sad sound echoing in the quiet office.

"Could you move so I could get to my...the desk? I want to finish and get out of here."

"If you stayed, we'd have a chance."

"A chance at what? At what, Parker? Hot sex and...more hot sex?"

His lips curled in a smile. "You make it sound so bad."

She tapped his arm to get him out of the way. Big mistake. In a flash, his large hand covered her arm and held tight. "Anna, please."

She closed her eyes. "Okay, fine. You're forgiven. Now move. I want to get out of here."

"I don't believe you."

"That's a problem we seem to have."

He eased her closer, close enough to smell the warm, spicy scent of aftershave. Close enough to see the individual whiskers of his beard growth and imagine the feel of it on her cheeks. Way, way too close.

"Anna, we can fix it. I made a mistake. I assumed the worst."

"Yes, I know." She nibbled at her lip, studying her desk instead of giving in to the temptation to look into his eyes. If she did, she'd be dead. He'd lean forward. He'd kiss her. She'd open her mouth and her heart and… "That's what really hurt me. You assumed the worst."

He slid his hand up her arm. "Anna, honey, I'm so sorry. I'm going to make it up to you." He dipped his head closer, his lips brushing her hair.

"No," she whispered. "You can't."

He pressed his mouth to her hair, her forehead, and tipped her chin up with one sure finger. "I can."

He could. Of course he could. He could have her in an instant because she was weak for him, weak down to the bone marrow.

As if he knew that, he moved in slow, confident motion, lowering his head, closing his eyes and then covering her mouth with an easy kiss of ownership. Instantly, every nerve ending sang. Her heart kicked against her ribs, a breath jammed in her chest, her arms went numb, her brain went black.

She opened her mouth as he slanted over hers, took his tongue and let him flatten her whole body against him, pinning her between him and the desk, growing harder and bigger against her.

His mouth was warm, tasting of mint and the distant

flavor of some foreign ale. Powerful, capable hands roamed her back and hips, pulling her into him. From deep in her chest, she heard her own voice moan his name softly. Liquid fire licked through her stomach, whipping down her veins, tightening and burning and aching for release.

While one of his hands gripped her backside, the other closed over her breast, her nipple instantly pebbling against the silk and the pressure.

His erection pulsed against her and all she could do was move into it, each arch of her body sending wicked, wild sparks down her spine and into her belly and between her legs.

He's your boss. He's your enemy.

He was Parker and she wanted him more than any man she'd ever met.

His fingers closed over the hem of her skirt, pulling it up over her thighs, higher and higher.

"Let me show you, Anna," he whispered into their kiss. "Let me."

She knew what he wanted and she wanted it, too. Her legs trembled as his fingers inched closer to the apex, closer to where she was already moist and ripe and ready.

She absolutely couldn't say no to him. But she had to. She had to.

He backed away at the first pressure of her hands on his shoulders. Slowly, as if he might hurt her if he moved too fast, he stood, giving her space with his body but holding her firm with his gaze. "Come home with me, Anna. We'll talk."

She almost laughed. "We will not talk. We'll…do this."

"Then we'll talk. Please, sweetheart. Please."

Sanity dripped back into her veins, slowly replacing the bubbling heat of desire. Was this what she wanted? Or was she just acting out another fantasy?

"You can't show someone how sorry you are with sex, Parker."

He closed his eyes. "I'm not just saying I'm sorry. I'm saying I...I...care for you, Anna. I—"

"Stop." God knows what he'd say to continue the sex at that point. "Don't go there, Parker. Don't make a mockery of love."

"I'm not—"

"Because I have practically loved you for three months—more. When I get weak and crazy at your touch it's not because you're so incredibly hot that I can't think— well, you are, but that's beside the point. It's because I've watched you, admired you, respected you for the whole time I worked for you."

"Anna, I—"

She held her hands up. "You didn't even know I existed until you found me undressed in your bathroom. And the minute you did, the next thing I knew it was London, champagne and foreplay. As soon as you suspected I was your spy, everything after that was a game to find out more."

"Actually, it wasn't."

"Actually, it was. And that's fine, Parker. But now that you know you're wrong, you can't just kiss me back into your bed until you get bored with me. No." She shook her head, her heart finally slowing to a normal beat, her brain and body finally composed.

"What could I do to prove you wrong, Anna?"

She thought about that, a pinch of a frown forming. "I can't even imagine. But I'm going home now. Alone." She reached for her package, but he took her arm.

"Anna, don't do this to us."

She stabbed two fingers into the straps of the sandals

he'd dropped on her desk and held them aloft. "There is no us, Parker."

And for the second time in one day, she squared her shoulders, raised her chin and walked away from the man she loved.

Only this time, she broke down and cried the minute she got in the elevator.

Parker stood next to Anna's desk for a long time, willing himself back to a state where he could think. His body didn't want to cooperate. It wanted to tear after that woman; promise the sun, moon and stars and then deliver. It wanted to throw her on the nearest flat surface and make love to her until she couldn't think about all the things he wished he could take back. He wanted to…

It didn't matter what his body wanted. Or his head.

For once, he had to think with his heart. Because if he couldn't do that for Anna Cross, the only woman he'd ever met whom he could really love, then he couldn't do it at all.

What could he possibly do to prove how he felt? He'd offered her the job back, he'd groveled apologies, he'd shown her how he felt.

There had been no ambivalence in her goodbye. That was it. He lost. He lost control. He lost focus. He lost…Anna.

With the thought squeezing his heart, he walked toward his office, unlocked it and stepped into the darkness. Moonlight streamed through the opened window, casting a white sheen all over the papers that he'd tossed in Anna's face, along with the bitter—and wrong—accusations. He bent and picked up the copy of the newspaper article, reading it, slowly.

It was all there. Allegations, accusations, implications.

No proof. Why hadn't he seen that? And why hadn't her boss set the record straight?

His gaze moved to the reporter's name, and the name of the newspaper. *The Indianapolis Star.* He pulled out his PDA and clicked on Barry Lynch's number. Parker wasn't going to sleep until he'd cleared Anna Cross's name. She might never give him another chance, but it was the only way he could think of to prove to her that he...

He did. He loved her.

What a time to figure that out.

Brown, beige, gray, tweed and taupe. It all went in one trunk to be shipped back to Indiana. Standing in her room, ankle deep in clothes, books, linens, shoes and a whole bunch of stuff she had somehow managed to squeeze into that tiny closet, Anna surveyed her little world and mentally calculated how long it would take to pack this up.

She had until the end of the month, but each day in the cheery little house in Coral Gables just made her less...cheery.

The doorbell rang and like a fool her hand hit her chest with the thought of Parker.

But she forced it away. He wouldn't show up at her house at nine-thirty in the morning, or the night or ever. She'd walked away and after a few days she'd stopped hoping he'd follow her. He'd abided by her decision. By now, he was probably halfway through his little electronic black book.

Still, she glanced in the mirror at the ponytailed, makeup-free image of a woman packing to move. Whoever it was, they'd see her like this. She wrenched the door open and burst into a squeal.

"Megan!"

"You quit your job?"

Anna drew back to let her friend in. "The decision was mutual. What are you doing here?"

Megan tossed her handbag onto a table. "I'm here to sign the contract and take the job. I called your office and some throaty thing named Sheila said you were no longer with the company, but if I needed Mr. Garrison, she would be happy to put me through." Megan did a dead-on imitation of Sheila and rolled her eyes.

Anna didn't even want to think about Sheila, or anyone, taking her place.

"I'm taking your 'run, don't walk' advice," Anna said, pulling Megan farther into the house. "And you're really taking the job?"

"I am." She glanced around at the boxes and empty shelves. "And where are you going?"

"Indiana."

"Oh, Anna. Why?" Megan dropped onto the sofa.

"I have to, Megan. I want to go up there and clear my name. I'm going to find my old boss, and hound the newspapers and force the truth to be told. I don't feel like I can do that from here."

Megan nodded. "I guess it's about time you did that. But, jeez, we're like ships passing in the night."

"I know," Anna agreed. "I can't believe I've been here four years and you're coming and I'm leaving."

Megan held up a hand. "Can you tell me exactly what happened to bring this on?"

"Remember the plan to find the culprit and win the CEO's undying affection and true love?"

"I didn't know we'd thrown true love into the mix, but, yeah. I remember the plan."

"It backfired."

"Oh." Megan looked truly sympathetic. "Make me coffee and tell me everything."

Anna did, and Megan listened from a seat at the kitchen table, asking a few insightful questions, but mostly letting Anna spew the whole painful story. Most of it, anyway. Some things just couldn't be shared. Shower encounters, for one.

"Wow, that was gutsy. Especially the showdown at the club. Too bad you didn't have any witnesses."

"Oh, I did," Anna said as she poured the coffee at the counter. "Stephen Garrison was right there and heard the whole thing."

When Megan didn't answer, Anna turned to see Megan fussing with the flower arrangement, gnawing her lip. "That must have been awkward," she finally said.

Anna put the mugs on the table and took a seat. "No, actually, it was great. But, later, in the office. That was…"

"Not so great?"

"That was the hardest thing I've ever done," Anna admitted. "I walked away from him and, God, Megan, I didn't want to. But I did what I had to do and I feel like a stronger woman because of it."

"Oh, God, I know that feeling."

Anna held her cup to her mouth, studying her friend over the rim. "You do?"

Megan pushed her chair back and suddenly looked around. "This place has real potential, you know. Have you ever thought of those beautiful white plantation shutters for those windows?"

"No, but I just had a brilliant idea," Anna said. "Why don't you move in here? You could take over the lease for me and I think the owner would consider lease to buy, but I never could afford that. This place would be perfect for you and Jade."

Megan's face lit up as the possibility took hold. "It would be. Especially with that fenced-in yard. She could get that puppy I've been promising her."

"I'll be out of here in a few days. We could just switch the lease over now. How long are you going to be in town?"

"Just today. I promised Jade I'd be back by tonight." Megan peered at the clock on the oven. "I just stopped by because I had a rental car and an hour to kill before I meet with my new partners." She grinned. "I like the sound of that."

"I bet you do," Anna agreed. "You'll be a fantastic partner. I see great things in your future."

They talked for a few more minutes, discussing how to switch the lease into Megan's name.

"Are you absolutely sure, Anna?" Megan asked. "You don't think you might change your mind and stay? You've made your point with Parker. Sometimes running isn't the best thing to do."

"I'm not running," Anna said. "I'm going up to straighten things out. I have to try and clear my name." She stood, hating the little lump in her throat that she got every time she thought about leaving. "But I might come back," she added. "You did."

Megan nodded and stood. "I'd better run to my new office. I'll call you later," she promised.

As they walked out to the driveway, both of them shielded their eyes against the blinding summer sunshine.

"Leave your winter coats at home," Anna said as they rounded the rental car. "In fact, leave them for me. I don't think I have any left."

They shared a warm embrace before Megan climbed in the car. "I wish you'd change your mind. I sure could use some friends down here," she said.

"You'll make friends so fast, Meg," Anna assured her. "Right now, I have to go back and do whatever I can to clear my name. I guess that means going up to Indiana to face my demons."

Megan hesitated before she pulled the door closed. "You know, Anna, if you really want to face your demons, maybe you ought to figure out where they are. I did."

She closed the door before Anna could ask what she meant. There was a clue there, Anna felt certain, but some things friends just didn't ask.

As Megan pulled out of the driveway, Anna waved once, then lifted her face directly toward the sun. She'd gotten so used to the warmth of Florida, the subtle changes that actually heralded seasons, even the constant humidity sort of felt like…home, now. Sure, her parents were still in Indiana, and that would always be her roots.

But she was a Miami girl now. On a sigh, she headed up the driveway and her foot bumped into something, making her stumble.

She looked down, surprised to see the newspaper that Megan must have just driven over. Frowning, she reached for it, certain she'd already brought the *Miami Herald* in a few hours ago.

As she unfolded it, she just stared at the words across the top. *The Indianapolis Star?*

Megan must have dropped it when she'd gotten out of the car. She must have had it with her on the plane. Anna skimmed the headlines, instantly transported back to her hometown.

The last time she'd read this newspaper, she'd been on the front page of the business section. She'd never picked up another copy, out of spite. She flipped the main section, passed Sports, and then stared at the word *Business* across the top, remembering the burn of humiliation and the physical pain the day that her picture had been right there in the left-hand column.

She froze and blinked. Was the sun playing tricks on her eyes? Because there it was...the same grainy picture. Was someone torturing her by giving her a copy of this paper?

Almost afraid, she let her gaze move to the headline, expecting time to stand still. Expecting to see the headline that ruined her life.

Local Businessman Reopens Corporate Espionage Case.

"Oh, my God," she whispered, clutching the newspaper tighter as she scanned the page for the date. Today's date.

Blood rushed in her head and her hands shook as she let herself read the words.

FiberTech CEO issued a statement yesterday...wrong party accused in five-year-old allegations...former venture capitalist charged with fraud and unlawful computer access...industrial espionage case that mistakenly focused on administrative assistant Anna Cross...Barry Lynch includes formal apology to former assistant...

She stood for a long time, letting the words and the realization melt her hardened heart while the south Florida sun warmed her whole body.

Parker. Parker had done this for her.

At the sound of a car door, she lowered the paper and slowly turned around.

Parker leaned against his convertible, his eyes hidden behind dark glasses, no smile on his handsome, chiseled face.

"I e-mailed them an updated picture," he said. "But they opted to go with what they had on file."

She opened her mouth to speak, but nothing came out.

He levered himself from the car and slid his sunglasses off, dropping them into his pocket. He wore a pale blue T-shirt, khaki shorts and light Top-Siders, like a Ralph Lauren model who'd just stepped off the golf course, his hair a little windblown, his face tan.

He was the most gorgeous thing she'd ever seen.

He took a few steps closer, a slow smile deepening, his beautiful clefted chin just a shadow in the sunlight.

"Barry Lynch asked me to deliver this to you." He reached toward her, holding an envelope.

Holding the newspaper with one hand, she took the envelope with the other. He'd talked to Barry Lynch. Her worst nightmare had taken place. And it had turned into a dream come true.

"It's his formal apology and a copy of the civil suit he's filed against Michael Montgomery," Parker told her. "They had a helluva time hunting that guy down."

She honestly didn't know what to say. "Oh. Parker."

He grazed her cheek with his knuckle. "That's Mr. Garrison to you."

"You did this." She held up the newspaper in one hand, the letter in the other. "You did all of this?"

"I had help. I have a good P.I. named Ace, of all things," he said with a smile. "And Lynch found me first. And—"

"But you made this happen."

He tilted his head in a gesture of acknowledgment and self-deprecation. "I did what any man would do for the woman...he..."

Her heart triple timed, then thudded to a near stop. He *what?*

But he didn't finish the sentence.

"Thank you," she said softly.

He reached toward her again, sliding his hand around

her neck and playfully giving her ponytail a tug. "I miss you, Anna."

That was what he meant. The woman he *misses*.

She closed her hand over his forearm. "I'm sure you're...busy at work."

He laughed softly, tunneling his fingers into the hair at her nape. "That's not why I miss you. Can I come in?"

"Of course...not."

"No?"

"If you come in, then..." She'd be in the shower, on the bed or on the floor in six minutes. Five. "I'll never get done packing."

His face fell. "Where are you going?"

"Indiana." She glanced down at the newspaper. Everything she'd wanted to do in Indiana was done. She looked up at him. "At least, I was going to Indiana. Now it doesn't seem I have to."

He practically exhaled with relief. "Of course not. You can stay."

"Parker," she said softly, almost laughing at his bone-deep belief that he could control everything. "You can't make all the decisions for the world or for me."

"No, I can't," he agreed. "But I need you here, Anna. I still have a corporate spy on the loose, a company in flux and a family in turmoil. I can't fix all those problems without you at my side, Anna."

At his side. As his administrative assistant. His lover, for a while, at least. And then what? She gave her head a definitive shake. "You'll find someone to help you. Sheila's already stepped in."

"I don't mean I want you at my side in the office, Anna."

His voice was so low and serious it sent a million chills down her back.

"You mean you want me in your bed," she said defiantly. "Don't you?"

"I mean I want you in my *life*. In my home. In my bed. In my heart. In my family. In my life." He pulled her closer, tilting her face toward his. "I love you, Anna. I don't want you just to work for Garrison, I want you to *be* a Garrison."

A spark of white-hot delight and disbelief popped in her heart. She blinked into the sun, into his deep brown eyes. "What?"

"Anna, you've changed me. You make me understand that not having control is fine. It's good. You make me believe that there is something far more important than business…. It's love. Anna, I love you. You're smart and sexy and kind and spirited and every bit as strong as I am. I want you to share my life and my name and even my whole, colorful family." He held her firmly, bringing her close to his chest and face to melt her with the fierceness of his focus and sincerity. "I want to marry you. I want to spend the rest of my life with you."

"Parker." His name on her lips was barely a whisper; her breath was so tight and her heart was pounding so hard she thought her chest would burst. "I've been in love with you for so long that I…I just don't know what to say."

"Start with *yes*."

"Yes."

"*I love you* is good. Try saying that."

She smiled. "I love you."

"Now tell me you'll marry me."

"I'll marry you."

"See?" He teased her closer with a flutter kiss. "That wasn't so hard."

"Parker," she repeated. "Let me do this on my own."

With a soft exhale, she slid her arms tighter around his neck and looked right into his eyes.

"Yes, I love you," she said. "And, yes, I want to marry you." She kissed him, slowly and softly at first, then he deepened their connection, lifted her off the ground and suddenly twirled her so fast, the newspaper fluttered all over the driveway.

"Don't leave me again, Anna," he crooned softly. "Don't go back to Indiana. You can pack, but I want you to move in with me. And we'll get married right away. A month, no more."

Joy spread through her whole being and she just clung to his powerful shoulders, warmed by the sun and so much love. "Parker, I can't believe this."

"Believe this." He squeezed her. "Believe me."

"I believe you," she assured him. "I just can't believe that I—I'm going to spend my whole life with you. I feel like I could just…oh." She couldn't grab hold of the right words, so she just tightened her grip on his arms. "I love you so much it hurts."

He laughed and kissed her. "It shouldn't ever hurt again, Anna. Now let's go inside, sweetheart. It's really hot out here."

"Okay," she agreed and then gave him a sly smile. "You still haven't seen my bedroom."

"I thought we'd start with the shower."

"Perfect." She beamed up at him. "Because I feel like singing."

"Oh, *nooooo*."

Laughing, she took him into her house to start making the music they both knew would last a lifetime.

* * * * *

**Every Life Has More
Than One Chapter**

Award-winning author Stevi Mittman delivers
another hysterical mystery, featuring Teddi Bayer, an
irrepressible heroine, and her to-die-for hero, Detective Drew Scoones. After all, life on Long Island can
be murder!

*Turn the page for a sneak peek
at the warm and funny fourth book,
WHOSE NUMBER IS UP, ANYWAY?,
in the Teddi Bayer series,
by STEVI MITTMAN.
On sale August 7.*

CHAPTER 1

"Before redecorating a room, I always advise my clients to empty it of everything but one chair. Then I suggest they move that chair from place to place, sitting in it, until the placement feels right. Trust your instincts when deciding on furniture placement. Your room should "feel right.""

—TipsFromTeddi.com

Gut feelings. You know, that gnawing in the pit of your stomach that warns you that you are about to do the absolute stupidest thing you could do? Something that will ruin life as you know it?

I've got one now, standing at the butcher counter in King Kullen, the grocery store in the same strip mall as L.I. Lanes, the bowling alley–cum–billiard parlor I'm in the process of redecorating for its "Grand Opening."

I realize being in the wrong supermarket probably doesn't sound exactly dire to you, but you aren't the one buying your father a brisket at a store your mother will somehow know isn't Waldbaum's.

And then, June Bayer isn't your mother.

The woman behind the counter has agreed to go into the freezer to find a brisket for me, since there aren't any in the case. There are packages of pork tenderloin, piles of spare ribs and rolls of sausage, but no briskets.

Warning Number Two, right? I should be so out of here.

But no, I'm still in the same spot when she comes back out, brisketless, her face ashen. She opens her mouth as if she is going to scream, but only a gurgle comes out.

And then she pinballs out from behind the counter, knocking bottles of Peter Luger Steak Sauce to the floor on her way, now hitting the tower of cans at the end of the prepared foods aisle and sending them sprawling, now making her way down the aisle, careening from side to side as she goes.

Finally, from a distance, I hear her shout, "He's deeeeeeaaaad! Joey's deeeeeaaaad."

My first thought is *You should always trust your gut.*

My second thought is that now, somehow, my mother will know I was in King Kullen. For weeks I will have to hear "What did you expect?" as though whenever you go to King Kullen someone turns up dead. And if the detective investigating the case turns out to be Detective Drew Scoones...well, I'll never hear the end of that from her, either.

She still suspects I murdered the guy who was found dead on my doorstep last Halloween just to get Drew back into my life.

Several people head for the butcher's freezer and I position myself to block them. If there's one thing I've learned from finding people dead—and the guy on my doorstep wasn't the first one—it's that the police get very testy when you mess with their murder scenes.

"You can't go in there until the police get here," I say, stationing myself at the end of the butcher's counter and in front of the Employees Only door, acting as if I'm some sort of authority. "You'll contaminate the evidence if it turns out to be murder."

Shouts and chaos. You'd think I'd know better than to throw the word *murder* around. Cell phones are flipping open and tongues are wagging.

I amend my statement quickly. "Which, of course, it probably isn't. Murder, I mean. People die all the time, and it's not always in hospitals or their own beds, or…" I babble when I'm nervous, and the idea of someone dead on the other side of the freezer door makes me very nervous.

So does the idea of seeing Drew Scoones again. Drew and I have this on-again, off-again sort of thing…that I kind of turned off.

Who knew he'd take it so personally when he tried to get serious and I responded by saying we could talk about *us* tomorrow—and then caught a plane to my parents' condo in Boca the next day? In July. In the middle of a job.

For some crazy reason, he took that to mean that I was avoiding him and the subject of *us*.

That was three months ago. I haven't seen him since.

The manager, who identifies himself and points to his nameplate in case I don't believe him, says he has to go into *his cooler*. "Maybe Joey's not dead," he says. "Maybe he can be saved, and you're letting him die in there. Did you ever think of that?"

In fact, I hadn't. But I had thought that the murderer might try to go back in to make sure his tracks were covered, so I say that I will go in and check.

Which means that the manager and I couple up and go in together while everyone pushes against the doorway to peer in, erasing any chance of finding clean prints on that Employees Only door.

I expect to find carcasses of dead animals hanging from

hooks, and maybe Joey hanging from one, too. I think it's going to be very creepy and I steel myself, only to find a rather benign series of shelves with large slabs of meat laid out carefully on them, along with boxes and boxes marked simply Chicken.

Nothing scary here, unless you count the body of a middle-aged man with graying hair sprawled faceup on the floor. His eyes are wide open and unblinking. His shirt is stiff. His pants are stiff. His body is stiff. And his expression—you should forgive the pun—is frozen. Bill-the-manager crosses himself and stands mute while I pronounce the guy dead in a sort of *happy now?* tone.

"We should not be in here," I say, and he nods his head emphatically and helps me push people out of the doorway just in time to hear the police sirens and see the cop cars pull up outside the big store windows.

Bobbie Lyons, my partner in Teddi Bayer Interior Designs (and also my neighbor, my best friend and my private fashion police), and Mark, our carpenter (and my dogsitter, confidant and ego booster), rush in from next door. They beat the cops by a half step and shout out my name. People point in my direction.

After all the publicity that followed the unfortunate incident during which I shot my ex-husband, Rio Gallo, and then the subsequent murder of my first client—which I solved, I might add—it seems like the whole world, or at least all of Long Island, knows who I am.

Mark asks if I'm all right. (Did I remember to mention that the man is drop-dead-gorgeous-but-a-decade-too-young-for-me-yet-too-old-for-my-daughter-thank-god?) I don't get a chance to answer him because the police are quickly closing in on the store manager and me.

"The woman—" I begin telling the police. Then I have

to pause for the manager to fill in her name, which he does: *Fran*.

I continue. "Right. Fran. Fran went into the freezer to get a brisket. A moment later she came out and screamed that Joey was dead. So I'd say she was the one who discovered the body."

"And you are…?" the cop asks me. It comes out a bit like who do I *think* I am, rather than who am I really?

"An innocent bystander," Bobbie, hair perfect, makeup just right, says, carefully placing her body between the cop and me.

"And she was just leaving," Mark adds. They each take one of my arms.

Fran comes into the inner circle surrounding the cops. In case it isn't obvious from the hairnet and bloodstained white apron with *Fran* embroidered on it, I explain that she was the butcher who was going for the brisket. Mark and Bobbie take that as a signal that I've done my job and they can now get me out of there. They twist around, with me in the middle, as if we're a Rockettes line, until we are facing away from the butcher counter. They've managed to propel me a few steps toward the exit when disaster— in the form of a Mazda RX-7 pulling up at the loading curb—strikes.

Mark's grip on my arm tightens like a vise. "Too late," he says.

Bobbie's expletive is unprintable. "Maybe there's a back door," she suggests, but Mark is right. It's too late.

I've laid my eyes on Detective Scoones. And while my gut is trying to warn me that my heart shouldn't go there, regions farther south are melting at just the sight of him.

"Walk," Bobbie orders me.

And I try to. Really.

Walk, I tell my feet. *Just put one foot in front of the other.*

I can do this because I know, in my heart of hearts, that if Drew Scoones was still interested in me, he'd have gotten in touch with me after I returned from Boca. And he didn't.

Since he's a detective, Drew doesn't have to wear one of those dark blue Nassau County Police uniforms. Instead, he's got on jeans, a tight-fitting T-shirt and a tweedy sports jacket. If you think that sounds good, you should see him. Chiseled features, cleft chin, brown hair that's naturally a little sandy in the front, a smile that…well, that doesn't matter. He isn't smiling now.

He walks up to me, tucks his sunglasses into his breast pocket and looks me over from head to toe.

"Well, if it isn't Miss Cut and Run," he says. "Aren't you supposed to be somewhere in Florida or something?" He looks at Mark accusingly, as if he was covering for me when he told Drew I was gone.

"Detective Scoones?" one of the uniforms says. "The stiff's in the cooler and the woman who found him is over there." He jerks his head in Fran's direction.

Drew continues to stare at me.

You know how, when you were young, your mother always told you to wear clean underwear in case you were in an accident? And how, a little further on, she told you not to go out in hair rollers because you never knew who you might see—or who might see you? And how now your best friend says she wouldn't be caught dead without makeup and suggests you shouldn't either?

Okay, today, *finally,* in my overalls and Converse sneakers, I get it.

I brush my hair out of my eyes. "Well, I'm back," I say.

As if he hasn't known my exact whereabouts. The man is a detective, for heaven's sake. "Been back awhile."

Bobbie has watched the exchange and apparently decided she's given Drew all the time he deserves. "And we've got work to do, so…" she says, grabbing my arm and giving Drew a little two-fingered wave goodbye.

As I back up a foot or two, the store manager sees his chance and places himself in front of Drew, trying to get his attention. Maybe what makes Drew such a good detective is his ability to focus.

Only what he's focusing on is me.

"Phone broken? Carrier pigeon died?" he asks me, taking in Fran, the manager, the meat counter and that Employees Only door, all without taking his eyes off me.

Mark tries to break the spell. "We've got work to do there, you've got work to do here, Scoones," Mark says to him, gesturing toward next door. "So it's back to the alley for us."

Drew's lip twitches. "You working the alley now?" he says.

"If you'd like to follow me," Bill-the-manager, clearly exasperated, says to Drew—who doesn't respond. It's as if waiting for my answer is all he has to do.

So, fine. "You knew I was back," I say.

The man has known my whereabouts every hour of the day for as long as I've known him. And my mother's not the only one who won't buy that he "just happened" to answer this particular call. In fact, I'm willing to bet my children's lunch money that he's taken every call within ten miles of my home since the day I got back.

And now he's gotten lucky.

"*You* could have called *me*," I say.

"You're the one who said *tomorrow* for our talk and then

flew the coop, chickie," he says. "I figured the ball was in your court."

"Detective?" the uniform says. "There's something you ought to see in here."

Drew gives me a look that amounts to *in or out?*

He could be talking about the investigation, or about our relationship.

Bobbie tries to steer me away. Mark's fists are balled. Drew waits me out, knowing I won't be able to resist what might be a murder investigation.

Finally he turns and heads for the cooler.

And, like a puppy dog, I follow.

Bobbie grabs the back of my shirt and pulls me to a halt.

"I'm just going to show him something," I say, yanking away.

"Yeah," Bobbie says, pointedly looking at the buttons on my blouse. The two at breast level have popped. "That's what I'm afraid of."

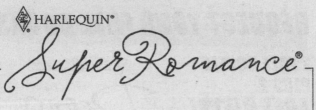

HARLEQUIN®

SuperRomance®

*Looking for a romantic, emotional
and unforgettable escape?*

*You'll find it this month and every month
with a Harlequin Superromance!*

Rory Gorenzi has a sense of humor and a sense of
honor. She also happens to be good with children.

Seamus Lee, widower and father of four, needs
someone with exactly those traits.

They meet at the Colorado mountain school owned
by Rory's father, where she teaches skiing and
avalanche safety. But Seamus—and his children—
learn more from her than that....

Look for

GOOD WITH CHILDREN

by Margot Early,

*available August 2007, and these other
fantastic titles from Harlequin Superromance.*

REQUEST YOUR FREE BOOKS!

2 FREE NOVELS PLUS 2 FREE GIFTS!

Passionate, Powerful, Provocative!

YES! Please send me 2 FREE Silhouette Desire® novels and my 2 FREE gifts. After receiving them, if I don't wish to receive any more books, I can return the shipping statement marked "cancel." If I don't cancel, I will receive 6 brand-new novels every month and be billed just $3.80 per book in the U.S., or $4.47 per book in Canada, plus 25¢ shipping and handling per book and applicable taxes, if any*. That's a savings of almost 15% off the cover price! I understand that accepting the 2 free books and gifts places me under no obligation to buy anything. I can always return a shipment and cancel at any time. Even if I never buy another book from Silhouette, the two free books and gifts are mine to keep forever.

225 SDN EEXJ 326 SDN EEXU

Name _____ (PLEASE PRINT)

Address _____ Apt. _____

City _____ State/Prov. _____ Zip/Postal Code _____

Signature (if under 18, a parent or guardian must sign)

Mail to the Silhouette Reader Service™:
IN U.S.A.: P.O. Box 1867, Buffalo, NY 14240-1867
IN CANADA: P.O. Box 609, Fort Erie, Ontario L2A 5X3

Not valid to current Silhouette Desire subscribers.

Want to try two free books from another line?
Call 1-800-873-8635 or visit www.morefreebooks.com.

* Terms and prices subject to change without notice. NY residents add applicable sales tax. Canadian residents will be charged applicable provincial taxes and GST. This offer is limited to one order per household. All orders subject to approval. Credit or debit balances in a customer's account(s) may be offset by any other outstanding balance owed by or to the customer. Please allow 4 to 6 weeks for delivery.

Your Privacy: Silhouette is committed to protecting your privacy. Our Privacy Policy is available online at www.eHarlequin.com or upon request from the Reader Service. From time to time we make our lists of customers available to reputable firms who may have a product or service of interest to you. If you would prefer we not share your name and address, please check here. ☐

SDES07

REASONS FOR REVENGE

A brand-new provocative miniseries by *USA TODAY* bestselling author **Maureen Child** begins with

SCORNED BY THE BOSS

Jefferson Lyon is a man used to having his own way. He runs his shipping empire from California, and his admin Caitlyn Monroe runs the rest of his world. When Caitlin decides she's had enough and needs new scenery, Jefferson devises a plan to get her back. Jefferson *never* loses, but little does he know that he's in a competition....

Don't miss any of the other titles from the REASONS FOR REVENGE trilogy by *USA TODAY* bestselling author **Maureen Child.**

SCORNED BY THE BOSS #1816
Available August 2007

SEDUCED BY THE RICH MAN #1820
Available September 2007

CAPTURED BY THE BILLIONAIRE #1826
Available October 2007

Only from Silhouette Desire!

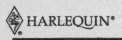
HARLEQUIN®

American | ROMANCE®

༺·TEXAS LEGACIES:·༻
ᵗʰᵉ CARRIGANS

Get to the Heart of a Texas Family

WITH

THE RANCHER NEXT DOOR
by
Cathy Gillen Thacker

She'll Run The Ranch—And Her Life—Her Way!

On her alpaca ranch in Texas, Rebecca encounters
constant interference from Trevor McCabe, the
bossy rancher next door. Rebecca becomes very
friendly with Vince Owen, her other neighbor and
Trevor's archrival from college. Trevor's problem
is convincing Rebecca that he is on her side, and
aware of Vince's ulterior motives. But Trevor has
fallen for her in the process....

On sale July 2007

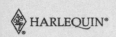

COMING NEXT MONTH

#1813 SEDUCED BY THE WEALTHY PLAYBOY—Sara Orwig
The Garrisons
She needed his help to rescue her sinking business…but didn't know his price would be the ultimate seduction.

#1814 THE TEXAN'S SECRET PAST—Peggy Moreland
A Piece of Texas
Starting an affair with his lady partner could have its perks, or it may reveal a truth best left hidden.

#1815 IN BED WITH THE DEVIL—Susan Mallery
Millionaire of the Month
She'd been the mousy girl he'd never looked at twice. Now she was the only woman he wanted in his bed.

#1816 SCORNED BY THE BOSS—Maureen Child
Reasons for Revenge
This millionaire thinks he can win his assistant back with seduction. Then she discovers his ploy and shows him two can play his game!

#1817 THE PLAYBOY'S PASSIONATE PURSUIT—Emilie Rose
Monte Carlo Affairs
He would stop at nothing to get her between his sheets… The race is on.

#1818 THE EXECUTIVE'S VENGEFUL SEDUCTION—Maxine Sullivan
Australian Millionaires
Five years of secrets and lies have built a wall between them. Is the time finally right for a passionate resolution?

SDCNM0707